THE LAST SOUNDS OF
CIVILIZATION . . .

Martina glanced around the school room. What she saw was a typical class—European history, from the look of the blackboard. She spotted a metal object on a nearby desk. It was a miniature tape recorder. She recalled Rosa telling her about a girl in her class who had a hearing impairment and taped all the lectures. Martina examined the machine. She hit "rewind," let it run for a few seconds, and then pressed "play."

She jumped at the sound of the teacher's voice. It was very clear, as if the teacher were right there in the room talking.

> *"With his first wife, Catherine of Aragon, Henry VIII had one child, Mary. When he decided to divorce his wife, in order to marry Anne Boleyn, he assumed that Anne Boleyn would produce a male heir, so he declared that . . ."*

The next sound was a gasp, a sharp intake of breath. This was followed by a faint shriek, and a jumble of unintelligible words and sounds. Then there was silence . . .

Other Avon Books in the
LAST ON EARTH *Trilogy*
by Marilyn Kaye
Coming Soon

BOOK TWO: THE CONVERGENCE
BOOK THREE: THE RETURN

LAST ON EARTH

BOOK ONE:

THE

VANISHING

MARILYN KAYE

AVON BOOKS ◆ NEW YORK

AVON BOOKS, INC.
1350 Avenue of the Americas
New York, New York 10019

Copyright © 1998 by Marilyn Kaye
Excerpt from *Last on Earth, Book Two: The Convergence* copyright
© 1998 by Marilyn Kaye
Published by arrangement with the author
Visit our website at **http://www.AvonBooks.com**
Library of Congress Catalog Card Number: 98-92788
ISBN: 0-380-79832-8

First Avon Books Printing: October 1998

AVON TRADEMARK REG. U.S. PAT. OFF. AND IN OTHER COUNTRIES, MARCA REGISTRADA, HECHO EN U.S.A.

Printed in the U.S.A.

WCD   10 9 8 7 6 5 4 3 2 1

For Cecile Chahid-Nouraï and Sebastien Clerc,
mes amies extraordinaires

prologue

at overcrowded madison High School, there was a shortage of classrooms, so fifth period geometry met in the basement, in what had been constructed as a bomb shelter when the school was built almost half a century ago. In this windowless, airless room, twenty-five seniors battled the drowsiness brought on by still air and heavy silence. Walls that were three feet thick obliterated the usual hum of footsteps and conversation that permeated the three floors above them. The only noise was the squeak of the chalk as Mr. Stark scrawled on the blackboard, and the soft scratch of pencils on paper as the students copied what he wrote.

"What time is it?" the teacher inquired.

The clock hanging above the blackboard couldn't provide an answer. Its hands hadn't moved since the term began, two weeks earlier. The sound of the school bells couldn't penetrate the concrete walls, so most of the students wore watches. Someone always had to remind Mr. Stark when it was time to change classes.

The first response to the teacher's question

came from Jake Robbins in the front row. "It's quarter after one," Jake told him.

"I need to make a phone call," Mr. Stark declared. "Excuse me, I'll be back in five minutes. You can look over your notes while I'm gone." Unlike the teachers at most other New York City high schools, he didn't threaten them with detention or worse if they behaved badly in his absence. Madison was a magnet school. Its students had been selected through general testing, and they all ranked in the upper third of public school students. It was assumed by many teachers that these kids were more mature and responsible than the average high school student and could be trusted to behave appropriately without adult supervision.

This was not a safe assumption. Upon Mr. Stark's departure, the class didn't erupt into chaos, but notebooks weren't studied either. Jake Robbins took out his journal, the one he carried around everywhere, and began to scribble. Martina Santiago and Donna Caparelli engaged in mild gossip. Several classmates leaned back in their seats or put their heads on their desks for a quick snooze. Ashley Silver listened to soft rock on a Walkman. Maura Kelly opened a makeup case and reapplied a coat of lipstick. David Chu attempted to use his cellular phone, but the room was too far underground for him to make a connection.

Others took advantage of the teacher's absence to stand up and stretch, or attempt a last-minute reading of whatever assignment was due next period. No one was particularly conscious of the passage of time until Travis Darrow spoke. "It's one thirty-five."

This meant that on the floors above them, a bell was ringing, indicating that it was time for all students to move on to their sixth-period classes. A couple of kids checked their own watches to confirm Travis's statement, but most didn't bother. As senior class president, Travis Darrow was notoriously reliable.

Obviously, Mr. Stark's telephone call had taken longer than he'd anticipated. Students began gathering books, jackets, whatever they'd brought with them. They couldn't wait for an official dismissal from the teacher, or they'd be late for their next class. They headed out of the classroom and up the stairs to the main floor of the school.

Days later, they would argue over who had the first sensation that something wasn't right. Some claimed they felt it on the stairs, but others insisted they became aware when the first person to reach the top of the stairs opened the door. At that moment, they should have been hit with a blast of noise—the din of over two thousand students changing classes, yelling, calling to each other. Feet stomping, doors slamming.

Instead, they were greeted by silence, and an empty hall.

Cameron Daley spoke first. "There must have been a fire drill."

That made sense to everyone. Back in their bomb shelter classroom, Mr. Stark had once remarked that he hoped there would never be a fire during fifth period. Every alarm and siren in the city could be wailing and they wouldn't hear anything.

"Nice of them to warn us," somebody grumbled as they moved toward the exit. The double doors were pushed open, and they all poured out onto the landing that overlooked the street. There, they stopped, and stood very still.

No one was out there. The normally busy Greenwich Village street was silent and deserted. The only sound was someone's breathless whisper, "What the hell . . ."

There were cars in the middle of the road, stranded and empty. A bus was poised at the curb with its door open, but no one was getting on or off. All along the sidewalks, there were things that must have belonged to people—shopping bags, bicycles, baby strollers. Above them, a plane hung in the air, motionless. It was as if time had stopped, the earth frozen on its axis.

And twenty-five high school seniors shared the sensation that they were bearing witness to the end of the world.

jake robbins stood in the kitchen of the home his family had occupied since before he was born. He'd never paid a great deal of attention to it, but as far as he could tell, it hadn't changed in any discernible way. The walls were still intact, and they were still green. Alongside the back door he'd come in through, the pencil marks charting his growth from the age of one were clearly visible. The geranium on the windowsill looked a little sickly, but it had probably always been like that. His mother didn't have much talent with plants.

The cabinet doors were closed, but he knew what he'd see if he opened them—stacks of plates (everyday and "good"), rows of glasses, bowls, and cups—all the items anyone would normally find behind cabinet doors in a kitchen. Everything was clean and neat. There were no dishes in the sink, no remnants of that morning's breakfast on the counter. His mother was an impeccable housekeeper, and she'd trained Jake and his father to comply with her belief that a home should always be ready for that unexpected visit from the President of the United States or British royalty.

This wasn't really necessary. Entertaining in

the Robbins family consisted mainly of Friday evening dinners or Sunday bagels and lox brunch with assorted aunts, uncles, and cousins, and maybe a neighbor or two.

Jake himself didn't entertain at all. As far as he knew, none of his classmates lived around here, in the neighborhood of Forest Hills in the borough of Queens. Even if they did, he probably wouldn't be entertaining them. He wasn't the social type.

He moved from the kitchen into the dining room. Again, nothing seemed peculiar or out of place. The dark wood of the table gleamed, the candlesticks were perfectly centered, and the chairs were positioned precisely. Above the table hung the elaborate chandelier which was taken down and polished just before Passover every year. Jake flicked the switch on the wall, but the chandelier didn't burst into light. So there was still no electricity. He couldn't say he'd expected any.

He looked at his digital watch. It read 1:35, the same time it had declared for—how long? It seemed like days, weeks even. But of course it had only been a couple of hours, maybe less, since his geometry class had left Madison High in search of . . . life.

There was no life in this house. He didn't even have to go upstairs and check the bedrooms to confirm this.

Of course, on an ordinary weekday afternoon at 1:35, there wouldn't be any life in this house. Jake would be at school in Manhattan. His mother and father would be a few blocks away, at the retail electronics store they owned and operated on Forest Hills's main shopping street. But Jake had already stopped by Robbins Electronics before coming home. They weren't there. No one was there. No one was anywhere.

In the living room, he sat down in his father's favorite armchair and mentally reconstructed the past hours. Like everyone else in his class, he'd left Madison almost immediately. Getting home hadn't been easy. He'd gone down into the nearby subway station, but there was no indication of any trains coming or going, and there were no other people on the platform. On the other side of the station, there *was* a train on the tracks. But it was empty, and going nowhere.

There were plenty of available cars on the streets above ground, with keys in their ignitions. But a turn of the key didn't produce any action. For Jake, it was the first indication that batteries weren't working. So he'd done what most of the other kids who didn't live nearby had done—he'd "borrowed" an abandoned bicycle and pointed it in the direction of home.

There were some signs of life, a dog here and there, a squirrel, a flock of birds, but nothing human. He'd maneuvered around the motionless cars on the 59th Street Bridge, pedaled through Jackson Heights and Kew Gardens, and didn't see one other person. The city was so still, he felt like he was moving through empty space.

Now he was home, but even that felt eerie, unreal. His eyes went to the mantel above the fireplace. There were the framed photos, mostly of him—Jake on the first day of kindergarten, Jake with a trophy that proclaimed him winner of a city-wide spelling bee, Jake as a bar mitzvah boy, Jake shaking hands with the borough president after winning an essay competition. Anyone looking at this display would know he was an only child, his parents' pride and joy. They had big dreams for him—a prestigious university, and then medical school or law school, something that could turn him into a professional. He'd been dreading the day when he would have to tell them he didn't want to be a doctor or a lawyer. Jake wanted to be a writer.

He knew what their reaction would be. His mother would weep, his father would yell: they would both wring their hands and wail at the mere notion that their brilliant and promising son should choose a career so insecure, so unreliable. It looked like he wouldn't have to worry about telling them now. . . .

The significance of what he was thinking hit him like a sharp punch in the stomach. Involuntarily, he cried out—and then he began to sob. Eventually the sobs turned into dry, choking coughs, and when that was over, he fell back into the armchair and tried to think clearly.

Jake's body was drained, but his mind raced with questions. What had happened? Why? Where was everyone? What was going to happen? What should he do, where should he go? Plenty of questions, no answers. He felt helpless. Well, at least he could move, and he did so just to assure himself that he was still real and alive. Jake rose from the chair almost violently, so quickly that he lost his balance, and had to reach out for the wall to steady himself. In doing this, his hand hit a light switch.

Two table lamps flickered, and then lit up. It took a moment for this to register in Jake's mind. He looked at his watch. The second hand was moving. So electricity and batteries were working now. For one wild and crazy moment, he could feel a surge of hope that sent him flying to the window. He pulled back the curtain and looked out onto the street.

Nothing else had changed. He let the curtain drop. Then his eyes rested on the remote control lying on top of the television. He picked it up and began pushing buttons.

For his father's birthday last year, Jake and his mother had presented him with his heart's desire, a satellite dish that could bring in five hundred channels from around the world. His father could live in video heaven, choosing between Brazilian soccer and Israeli soap operas. But today, Jake couldn't locate anything; at least, not anything that moved. On one channel, he saw the set of a news program, with a weather map. But no one stood in front of it.

On another channel, he had the view of a street. From the street signs, he knew he was seeing a locale in France, or maybe Quebec. It didn't matter. No one was walking on those streets either. He kept punching the remote. Sometimes he saw blank screens, sometimes an arena, a stadium, a stage set. No people. It was weird, seeing a football field with no players, bleachers devoid of fans. After a while, he had to believe what he was already suspecting—that there was no one, anywhere, in the whole wide world, with the exception of twenty-five seniors from Madison High.

He couldn't stay there. He ran up to his room, and began stuffing things into his backpack— some underwear, a couple of T-shirts, a sweater, a toothbrush. He tossed in a copy of *The Catcher in the Rye* and the spiral notebook he used as a journal. He was filled with an inexplicable sense of urgency, as if he had to get out of the house fast.

But once outside the front door, he just stood there, at the top of the steps leading to the sidewalk.

He had no idea where he was going.

Martina closed the door of her family's third-floor apartment and carefully bolted the two double-locks. Going through the ritual motion wasn't particularly comforting, but she didn't know what else to do. From what she'd seen on the downtown streets as she ran home from Madison, no one would be breaking into the apartment.

Martina didn't live that far from school. It was only a twenty-minute bus ride from her family's apartment on Manhattan's Lower East Side to Madison High in Greenwich Village. On nice days, when she hadn't overslept and wasn't running late, she could walk the distance in half an hour.

It seemed to take longer today, maybe because she was stopping constantly, peering through store windows and down side streets, hoping to see somebody. Or maybe it was because she was walking alone, when she usually walked to school with her twin sister, Rosa.

She didn't see another human being until she returned to Madison High. There she noticed her classmate, Kesha Greene, sitting alone on the steps leading to the main entrance doors. Martina climbed the stairs and sat down just below Kesha. "What are you doing here?" she asked.

"I didn't know where else to go."

It was strange, hearing uncertain words like that coming from the tall, good-looking Black girl with her strong features and thick African-style braids. She had always seemed like the kind of person who knew what she was doing, where she was going. Martina couldn't say she knew Kesha well, but like most students at Madison, she was aware of her as a school activist, busy and involved. She had a reputation for being opinionated, passionate. Martina had always found her a little intimidating.

She didn't seem so intimidating now.

"Where have you been?" Martina asked her. "Did you see anyone?"

"Uptown, Harlem," Kesha replied in answer to the first question. For the second, she merely shook her head.

"Harlem," Martina repeated. "That's a long way from here."

"I walked up, but I drove back."

"You found a car that worked?"

Kesha nodded. Martina looked at her watch. It was running again, and it read 2:05. But that didn't really mean anything to her, since she had no idea how long time had been standing still.

She jumped at the sound of a door opening behind her, and turned to see a small, thin boy with wire-rimmed glasses standing there. It took Martina a minute to remember his name. "Hi, Cameron." It seemed like an oddly natural greeting in such an unnatural situation, but what else was there to say?

"Hi," he said, and then he looked up.

Martina glanced at the sky, but she didn't see anything special. "What are you looking at?"

"There was a plane up there," Cameron said. "It's gone now."

"I guess it flew away."

"I don't think so," Cameron said.

"Then it landed," Kesha said. "Or it crashed."

The boy shook his head. "If it had crashed we would have heard something." He frowned. "There must have been other planes in the air too. There should be fires. I guess the planes just stopped, like those cars."

"But the cars are still there, and the planes are gone," Kesha pointed out. "Why is that?"

Cameron looked at her pityingly. "You don't really expect me to answer that. I might be your class techno nerd, but I don't know what happened."

"A bomb?" Martina wondered.

"But all the buildings are standing," Kesha said.

"There are new weapons," Cameron said. "Chemical ones, lasers. I've read about them. They only destroy people."

"Then where are the bodies?" Kesha asked.

"Disintegrated?" Cameron proposed. "Dissolved, evaporated? I don't know, something like that, I guess."

Kesha spoke sharply. "This isn't an *Amazing Adventures* action comic, Cameron."

"I know that," Cameron replied.

"Someone's coming," Martina announced. She squinted at the figure on the approaching bike. "Oh. She's in our class."

Kesha jumped up. "It's Donna Caparelli!" She waved. "Donna!"

The bike wobbled to a halt in front of the school steps. Donna got off and joined them on the steps.

"Did you go home?" Martina asked her.

Donna shook her head. "I live on Staten Island. The ferry's not running."

"You could bike into Brooklyn and take the Verrazano Bridge," Cameron suggested.

Donna shrugged. "What's the point?" She sat

down by Kesha and rested her head on the taller girl's shoulder. Kesha put an arm around her. Martina couldn't help feeling a little envious of their close friendship. If Rosa were there, they could be comforting each other. She found herself watching the street eagerly, as if her twin would appear any moment. But Rosa hadn't been in her geometry class. And it was only those classmates who began returning to the school.

They came, one by one, from different directions. Some walked with a purpose, others drifted aimlessly. Some arrived breathless, frightened, in a panic. Others moved like sleepwalkers or zombies. They came back because it was the one place where they might encounter another human being. They shared what little they knew. No one had seen anybody else—not uptown, or downtown, not in the Bronx or in Queens. One kid lived in a West Side highrise with a view over the Hudson River. He hadn't seen anything moving in New Jersey.

Eventually there was nothing left to say or tell, and they all sat quietly, lost in their own thoughts and fears. The silence of the city hung over them like a thick, heavy blanket, so heavy Martina felt like she was suffocating. She wanted to break the silence, if only to make noise, but she couldn't think of anything to say.

Finally, someone else did. Alex Popov got up suddenly. "I'm not going to sit here and do nothing."

Donna looked at him quizzically. "What are you going to do?"

"Make a long-distance phone call. Whatever happened, maybe it's just around here. Somebody's gotta be out there somewhere."

"Need some change?" a boy asked.

"Nah, I got a phone card." He started up the stairs to the main doors. The tiny Indian girl who rarely spoke in class also stood. "May I come? I want to make a phone call, too."

Alex shrugged, and the girl followed him into the building.

After a couple of minutes, Donna made a proposition. "Maybe we all should go inside. If there was a bomb, we could be getting hit with a lot of radioactivity right now."

"The building won't protect us," Cameron informed her. "We'd have to go back down to the bomb shelter. Anyway, we've already been exposed."

Maura Kelly's voice quavered. "How long do we have?"

"There's no way of telling. We don't have enough information," Cameron told her. When Maura proceeded to burst into tears, Cameron amended his comment quickly. "Hey, don't jump to conclusions. We don't know if there's any radiation in the air, we don't even know if there was a bomb."

"What does it matter?" a girl asked. "You want to go on living if everyone else is dead?"

"Don't talk like that!" Martina said sharply.

Alex came out of the building, followed closely behind by the small dark-haired girl. "I called my great-aunt at her nursing home in California," he said. "There was no answer."

"What about you?" Kesha asked the girl. "What's your name?"

"Shalini Chatterjee," she replied softly. "I called my grandmother."

"She didn't tell me she was calling India," Alex

said in an aggrieved tone. "She could have used up my whole phone card."

"No time gets used up if no one answers," Cameron said.

"How do you know no one answered?" Kesha challenged him.

Cameron turned to Shalini. "Did anyone answer?"

She shook her head. "I tried to call my aunt, too. And a cousin."

"Maybe they just weren't home," someone suggested.

Shalini looked at her watch. "It is early in the morning in India. They should be at home."

"Wait a minute," Donna said. "Did you actually hear a phone ringing? Then there has to be someone out there! Or else you'd just get a dead line."

"Not necessarily," Cameron said. "Phones are on automated systems. They could go on working for a while without any people operating them."

Again, Martina looked at him in annoyance. "How can you talk like that? How can you sound so calm?"

Cameron squinted at her through his glasses. "I'm just stating facts," he said mildly.

Martina shivered. "I'm cold," she said to no one in particular. She realized that her jacket was still in her locker inside. The same thought must have occurred to others. They all began going inside. As if by unspoken agreement, they made their way downstairs to the cafeteria.

A boy stood in front of one of the snack machines that lined the wall. "Anyone got change for a dollar?"

David Chu sneered at him. "I can't believe

you're wasting your time on that crap," he muttered. A few seconds later, as he was leaving the cafeteria with a couple of guys, he stopped near Martina and eyed her curiously.

"Rosa?"

"No," she said coldly. "I'm Martina."

"Oh yeah, right. Rosa wasn't in that class."

"No," Martina said. "She wasn't."

He moved on with his friends. Martina gazed after him with distaste. She and Rosa were pretty much identical, but close friends could tell who was who. David had been going strong with her sister Rosa that summer; they'd been practically inseparable for three months, but he still couldn't tell them apart. He hadn't even noticed whether his former girlfriend was in his class. What a beast.

Someone thrust an open bag of chips in Martina's face. "Want some?"

"No, thanks." How could anyone think of food at a time like this? But it appeared that even the most horrendous, unspeakable disasters couldn't kill some appetites. At least a dozen kids were poking quarters into machines, gathering sodas, potato chips, candy bars. Others were sitting quietly with one other person, or two. Martina felt very alone.

She made her way over to a table where another lone female figure sat in a huddled position. She knew who the girl was, of course. Ashley Silver was the closest thing Madison had to a celebrity.

"Hi, Ashley," Martina said.

The girl looked up. She was strikingly beautiful, with skin the color of café au lait, black eyes, and fair hair that hung to her shoulders in a cloud of curls. She didn't speak.

"I saw your picture in *Seventeen* this month. You looked great in that gown."

Still, Ashley said nothing. She just stared at Martina like she didn't know what she was talking about. Martina made one more effort.

"I'm going to get something out of the machines. You want anything?"

"No."

Martina wasn't surprised. Ashley was a professional model, and she probably never ate anything. She never spoke to the ordinary mortals at Madison either. The world coming to an end was no reason for her to start talking now. Once a snob, always a snob.

Martina walked away. Back on the other side of the cafeteria, a boy was kicking one of the candy machines. "Damn machine ate my money," he muttered.

"This is really stupid," another boy said. "Why are we putting money into these things?" He picked up a chair and threw it at the candy display. The glass shattered, and kids began scrambling for candy. Within seconds, the other machines were broken into, and people were stuffing candy bars into pockets, bags of chips into handbags. Maura and another girl made a dash for the last diet soda can that was rolling on the floor. As they were both about to pounce on it, Maura shoved the other girl, hard. Someone else cried out in outrage as a bag of pretzels was ripped from his hands.

"Stop it!" Kesha shrieked. "You're acting like animals!"

A fight broke out. Martina edged alongside the wall, watching her classmates in horror. Of course, they weren't all involved. She saw Travis Darrow sitting at a table with a couple of other guys, watching the ruckus with wide eyes. Why couldn't Travis do something, she wondered. After all, he was the president of the senior class. People had voted for him, they must respect him. But she guessed that in a situation like this, his title didn't pull much weight. They needed a principal, a school security guard, a police officer, someone with real authority. Only there weren't any people like that around.

A distraction came, though not in the way Martina would have liked. David Chu and his friends reappeared, lugging cases of beer. "Come and get it!" David yelled, and kids fell on the cases like parched desert travelers at an oasis.

"Where did they get all that beer?" she wondered out loud.

Kesha and Donna were standing nearby and heard her. "Anywhere," Kesha told her. "There are hundreds of stores that sell beer. And nobody's minding them. They can walk in anywhere and take anything they want."

A couple of kids shook bottles of beer and opened them, sending streams of foam into the air. Someone had brought in a portable cassette player, and a blast of music filled the cafeteria. It was the band R.E.M., and a few kids started singing along with the song "It's the end of the world as we know it."

Martina wanted to get out of there. She could go to the school library, or the teachers' lounge, where there was a sofa she could lie down on. But the thought of being alone was even more horrifying than the reality of being here. So she slid down the wall onto the floor. She drew her knees up to her chest, wrapped her arms around her legs, and waited for the world to end completely.

two

Jake opened his journal to the first clean page. At the top of the sheet he wrote *Thursday, October 8*. Then he lifted the pen and looked at the date. Was he sure about that? It would be very easy to lose track of days and times.

It shouldn't be hard, counting back. His last journal entry had been on September 29. It had been brief, something about having finished a scorching editorial on politically apathetic youth for the *Madison Monitor*. The piece was due on the 30th. That was the day before it happened, so that day must have been the 31st. No, wait, "Thirty days hath September . . ." He really should get a calendar. Or better yet, write in his journal every morning and note the date there. He couldn't have control over much in this world anymore, but at least he could know what day it was.

Now he had to concentrate. He had to record on paper the events of an entire week. He supposed he could go out and get a state-of-the-art personal computer to write on, the kind he could never afford before. But he found the old-fashioned way oddly comforting. And right now he neeeded all the comfort he could get.

He closed his eyes and forced the images of one week ago to flash back into his head. It was all pretty fuzzy . . . the empty house in Forest Hills, the vacant streets, the unreal silence of New York. He remembered returning to Madison that evening, hoping to find classmates there. He'd found most of them gathered in the cafeteria. Some were drunk, others might have been sober but seemed drunk in their hysteria. Some people were crying, some were fighting, and others just sat alone, frozen, staring at nothing. He had a vague recollection of someone singing, off-key, that old Prince song, the one about the world ending in 1999, and there's nothing you can do about it so you might as well party. He remembered wanting to get away from them, but not too far. So he'd gone down the hall to the school gymnasium, where he'd fallen asleep on an exercise mat.

When I woke up the next morning, I was confused and disoriented. And hungry. According to my watch, it was six in the morning, but I didn't know if the watch was working. I went into the boys' locker room, where I took a shower—thank goodness, the plumbing still worked.

Coming out of the locker room, he encountered two girls with wet hair emerging from the showers on the other side. He recognized both of them, but he only knew the Black girl's name.

"Hi, Kesha," he said.

"You're Jake, right?"

He nodded.

She indicated her companion. "You know Donna?"

"Hi, Donna."

Donna gave him a "pleased to meet you" smile. "You write those editorials for the *Monitor*, don't you? They're good."

"Thanks."

Then the three had looked away, as if realizing at the same time how bizarre it was, having what sounded like a normal school hallway conversation, under the circumstances.

"I wonder why the plumbing still works," Donna said. Nobody answered her. Together, they walked to the cafeteria and stayed together in the entrance, taking in the scene silently.

Sleeping bodies were huddled on the floor. There was a foul smell in the air, like the morning after an all-night party, cigarette smoke and stale beer and vomit. They wandered through the school, locating others sleeping in restrooms, the teachers' lounge, the reception area outside the principal's office. Then, as if by unspoken agreement, they left the building.

Nothing had changed outside. We crossed the street, and went to a coffee shop. We scrambled eggs and fried bacon, and we started to feel a little more human. It felt good not being alone. Kesha's a pretty tough girl. I knew who she was because she's always writing angry letters to the Monitor, to protest compulsory phys ed classes, and to demand new courses in feminist studies, African American literature, Eastern Civilization. She always looks angry.

Her friend, Donna, is softer, sweeter, a more romantic type. When we left the coffee shop, she stopped to play with a cat.

"Oh, the poor little thing," Donna crooned, crouching down to stroke the kitten, who rubbed against her leg and made crying sounds. "He must be hungry."

"If he's hungry enough he'll find something to eat," Kesha said. But that didn't stop Donna from running across the street to a bodega, and bringing back a can of cat food.

"There are going to be a lot of hungry animals around," Kesha told her. "You can't feed all of them."

"Not to mention all the hungry people," Jake said.

"There won't be that many hungry people," Kesha said. "How many of us were in that class? Twenty-five?"

Donna gave the cat one more stroke, and rose. "Do you really think we're the only people in the world?"

"Looks like it," Kesha said, with an attitude of bravado she couldn't quite pull off.

The stillness was broken by two barking dogs, running down the street, dragging their leashes. Donna turned to Jake. "Why are all the animals still around, but not the people?"

Jake shrugged. "I don't know."

"Nobody knows, Donna," Kesha said. She mimicked Donna's soft voice. "Why is the electricity working? Where did everyone go?" Her voice went back to normal. "I wish you'd stop asking questions that no one can answer."

We wandered around for a while, and then we came to a building, just on the edge of Soho, that Donna knew. At least, she'd read about it. It was an old building that had just been renovated as a hotel. It was supposed to be homey and old-fashioned, not like the high-rise glitzy hotels in midtown. We went in and looked around. The keys to the rooms were available at the reception desk, so we looked into some of them. They were nice, not too fancy, but cheerful, with bright colors and clean bathrooms. Everything worked, like plumbing and electricity. It was Kesha who came up with the bright idea of moving in. There were enough rooms for everyone in the geometry class to have a private room.

Jake didn't find the idea wildly appealing. "You really want to stay together? Why? It's not like we're all great buddies."

Donna also was puzzled by Kesha's suggestion. "Do you realize who you'll be living with? There are some real macho jerks in that class. Kyle Bailey, Mike Salicki, you can't stand those guys."

"Travis Darrow," Jake added, and Kesha grimaced. Last spring, when they were all juniors, Kesha had run for senior class president against Travis. When Travis won, Kesha wrote a letter to the *Monitor* blaming his victory on rampant sexism. She couldn't use racism as an excuse since Travis was Black.

"I can deal with that," Kesha said. She spoke meaningfully to Donna. "Can you?"

Donna went a little pink. "That's all over with,

and you know it." From this, Jake drew the conclusion that Donna and Travis had once been in a relationship. But he didn't see what this had to do with the larger issue.

"We've got a whole city out there," he told Kesha. "Forget about private rooms, we can each have our own building!"

Kesha shook her head. "I think we need to stay together, for a while at least. We don't know what happened, we don't know what's going to happen. There's safety in numbers. We could look out for each other."

So we went back to Madison, and told the kids about the hotel. We put up signs telling everyone else where we were. A couple of kids went home to get some personal stuff. Others picked up things they needed in stores along the way. Some guys were acting like this was their one and only chance to stock up. They were looting, grabbing everything they could carry. Who was going to stop them?

Jake stopped writing then. He'd come to the part he didn't want to think about, the fact that they all had the potential to turn into uncivilized savages. Come to think, he could make a whole list of topics he didn't want to think about. His parents, his best pal Ian, that cute sophomore, Kate something, who'd just joined the *Monitor* staff, all the people who were gone. No one was talking about them. It was as if an unwritten law had been declared—there shall be no speaking of the past. A new world had been created on the first of October. And they were acting as if nothing had come before.

Or maybe he was just being dramatic. Maybe people weren't ready to talk about anything yet; they were still feeling their way, trying to adjust. Maybe he needed to get out of this room and stop thinking in general.

He went out into the hall, and considered asking someone to go for a walk with him. There were three other rooms on his hallway, but he didn't know any of the occupants very well. He'd exchanged a few words with the guy just across from him, Andy Loomis. He was about to rap on Andy's door when another door opened.

Ashley Silver came out of her room. She didn't speak as she passed Jake, though he could have sworn he saw her eyelids flicker in recognition. Her face was vague and expressionless. She was like a zombie, but still so pretty.

Now Andy opened his door. His hair was tousled and he wore nothing but flowered boxer shorts. "Hi, beautiful," he said to Ashley. But Ashley floated by without acknowledging him, and disappeared into the stairwell.

Andy turned to Jake. "She's a babe, huh?" he said appreciatively. "What's her problem?"

"Still in shock, I guess," Jake replied.

Andy shrugged that off. "Who isn't? Too bad about *her*, though. Most of the girls here, I couldn't care less if they're in permanent shock. But I wouldn't mind a little communication with her, if you know what I mean."

Jake nodded. He knew what Andy meant.

"She's a professional model, right?" Andy asked.

"Yeah, that's what I've heard."

"Then she's probably being a snob."

"I don't know," Jake said. "Maybe she's just depressed."

"Can't blame her," Andy remarked. "She must have had a great life, before. It has to be tough, losing all that."

"It's tough for everyone," Jake said.

Andy yawned. "I dunno. I'm doing okay." He grinned. "Sleep all day, party all night. No midterms. What else could a guy ask for?" He went back into his room.

Interesting question, Jake thought. What else could a guy ask for? How about a home, a family, a future?

Then he had to smile. What was it Kesha had said—something about how useless it was to ask questions no one could answer? Maybe Andy had the right attitude.

three

martina santiago was asleep, and dreaming about a mirror.

It wasn't a deep sleep, just the sort of half-doze that happens when you lie down for a nap in the middle of the afternoon. She knew she was dreaming, so she wasn't at all alarmed when her reflection in the mirror reached out to take her hand. Then she realized that the image in the mirror wasn't a reflection at all, but the face of her sister Rosa. Martina was pleased to see her sister, but surprised to find her there.

"Rosa, what are you doing in my mirror?" she asked.

Rosa didn't answer. She didn't smile either. But her grip on Martina's hand tightened, to the point where it was almost painful. With some regret, Martina forced her eyes open. She found her own hands clasped together, her right hand's fingernails digging into her left hand. When she let go, she could see faint crescents on her left palm.

She sat up, and shook her head briskly. She'd been having a lot of weird dreams like this lately. Maybe it had something to do with the fact that she was sleeping alone in the room. Or maybe it was the bed. Before, in another room, in another life, she had slept on a single bed, with Rosa on an identical bed against the opposite wall. In this queen-size bed, Martina felt lost.

She went into the bathroom to splash some water on her face. Now that she was fully awake, she wasn't sure what to do. Other kids she knew were running all over the city. Martina had a tendency to stick close to the hotel. She'd been a homebody before, too. Rosa had been much more adventurous than she was.

She felt a pang, the one that hit in the middle of her stomach every time she thought about her sister. Picking up a brush, she pulled it violently through her hair, as if she could brush thoughts of her sister right out of her head. She shouldn't go on feeling sorry for herself. Everyone here was missing somebody, sisters, brothers, parents, friends. Lovers. For once, Martina could be grateful for never having had a serious boyfriend.

But she had a sister, one who was more than a sister. Nobody here could understand what kind of relationship identical twins have. It wasn't just loss that she felt. It was as if half of herself was missing.

She decided to go to a bookstore she and Rosa used to frequent, on Tenth Street, about a fifteen-minute walk from here. That would give her a destination, and a purpose—she could use something new to read.

She ran into Donna Caparelli in the lobby. "Hi," Donna said brightly. "What's up?"

Funny, how they were still using expressions like this with each other, as if nothing had changed. Martina played along. "Nothing much. I'm going to a bookstore. What are you up to?"

"I'm waiting for Kesha. I don't know what we're going to do. Want to hang out with us?"

She knew she needed to make some friends here. She couldn't keep relying on dream conversations with Rosa. "Okay."

The tall, handsome Black teenager strode into the lobby with the same assurance Martina had seen her demonstrate coming into class, before. Together the three girls left the hotel.

"I need to get some stuff at the drugstore," Kesha said, so they turned right, in the direction of a large pharmacy. They reached a wide avenue, and Martina automatically paused, looking left and right before crossing.

"What are you doing?" Donna asked her.

Embarrassed, Martina tried to laugh. "I forgot."

As they passed a trendy shop, Maura Kelly came running out. "Guys, look!" She dangled a dress in front of them. It was black, with beads and rhinestones. "Isn't this gorgeous? And it fits perfectly. Look at the price tag."

Donna read the price out loud. "One thousand, two hundred."

"Can you believe that?" Maura laughed. "Have you ever owned something that cost so much? It's so perfect!" Clutching the dress close, Maura ran back in the direction of the hotel.

Donna grinned. "Perfect for what? Does she think we're actually going to have a senior prom this year?"

They arrived at the drugstore. "What do you need?" Donna asked Kesha.

Kesha pulled a list from her jeans pocket. "Aspirin. Tampons. Toilet paper. Shampoo."

"I need some dental floss," Donna said.

Kesha raised her eyebrows. "Dental floss?"

"None of us are going to be seeing a dentist any time soon," Donna said. "We have to take care of our teeth. Do you need anything, Martina?"

"I'm almost out of toothpaste," Martina said. "And I'll probably see some other stuff I need."

They picked up shopping baskets and began cruising down an aisle. Martina noticed some of the shelves were beginning to look a little bare. She wondered how many pharmacies there were in New York.

Kesha had moved on ahead. "What about condoms?"

Donna laughed. "What about them?"

"Well, I don't need them, but maybe we should have some around. In case anyone else needs them."

"Like who?" Donna asked. "Maura and David?"

Kesha snorted. "She wishes."

"Is something going on between Maura and David?" Martina asked.

"Only in Maura's head," Donna said. "Like half the other girls at school."

Martina didn't say anything, but her expression must have revealed something, because Kesha eyed her curiously. "Okay, who do you want to kill, Maura or David?"

Martina was taken aback. But the apparent keen interest of both Kesha and Donna encouraged her to speak. "He used to go with my sister, Rosa." The sympathy on their faces told her they were both well aware of David's reputation.

Kesha spoke bluntly. "And he broke her heart, right?"

"She was devastated," Martina admitted. "She never got over it."

"David Chu is serious scum," Kesha stated.

Donna shook her head sympathetically. "Why do girls fall for worthless guys like that?"

Kesha looked at her meaningfully. "You should know."

Now it was Martina's turn to look curious. Donna explained, "I used to go with Travis Darrow, and Kesha won't ever let me forget it." To Kesha, she said, "It's ancient history, girlfriend. Give me a break."

Martina didn't know Travis, but she certainly knew *of* him. "Were you together for very long?"

"We started going together last February," Donna told her. She smiled ruefully. "I'd had a crush on him for ages."

"Did your parents mind?" Martina asked curiously. "Because of the racial difference?"

"If they had known, they would have hit the roof," Donna said. "My father's not exactly Mr. Liberal. If he found out I was dating a Black guy, I don't know who he would have killed, me or him."

"When did you break up?"

"May, just before the class elections. I got this feeling he'd only been dating me for political reasons. You know, so people wouldn't think he was an Upper East Side snob." Her tone was bitter and wistful at the same time. "Travis thought that he could be the first Black president of the United States. I don't think he envisioned a white, working-class Italian girl from Staten Island as his first lady."

Martina couldn't argue with this. Travis came from an important family. His father was a senator, and a couple of years ago, a photo of the entire Darrow family had appeared in *Time* magazine.

"I could never figure out what Travis was doing

at Madison," Kesha remarked. "The Darrows are super rich; they live on Park Avenue. Why doesn't he go to one of those ritzy prep schools uptown?"

"His father thinks it's better for him politically to send his son to a public school," Donna said.

It occured to Martina that they were speaking in the present tense, as if they were all still going to Madison High and living at home with their families. But how else could they talk?

When they finished in the pharmacy, they left the store, passing the cash register on the way. Martina wondered if she'd ever get used to not paying for anything anymore.

But apparently, some people weren't having any problem getting used to that. From where they stood, they could see the broken glass on the sidewalk in front of a record store. Then two boys ran out the door with armfuls of compact discs.

Kesha squinted. "That looks like Kyle Bailey. I can't see the other one."

"Why are they doing that?" Donna wondered. "I'm sure the door to the place was open. They could have walked in, picked what they wanted, and left."

"They want to act like gangsters," Kesha said. "They're having a good time. Bunch of jerks."

"Sad, isn't it," Donna commented. "All those great guys, gone, and we're left with people like Kyle Bailey and David Chu."

"And Travis Darrow," Kesha added.

"Oh, come on, Kesha," Donna remonstrated. "You can't put Travis in the same category as Kyle and David. He's not that bad."

Kesha rolled her eyes. "I can't believe you still have feelings for him."

Donna shrugged. "Look, I'm not pining away for

Travis. I know he's shallow and egocentric and incapable of really loving anyone but himself. But it's not easy to stop caring about someone, even when you know it isn't going to happen."

"That's what my sister says about David," Martina said.

Donna smiled. "I'll bet you understand what I mean."

"Is it true what they say about identical twins?" Kesha asked Martina. "That you have some sort of special way of communicating, and you know what the other one is thinking?"

"Sometimes," Martina admitted. "I remember one day last summer, when we were at a family picnic. Rosa was off playing with a little cousin. Suddenly, I felt something sharp, like a bite, on my right hand. I thought I'd been stung by a bee, but there was nothing on my hand. Then Rosa came back, furious, because the bratty cousin had bitten her—on her right hand."

"Maybe you just didn't see the bee," Donna proposed. "Or the sting didn't leave a mark."

"I guess that's possible," Martina acknowledged. "But there are other things. Like we get headaches at the same time. Or I'll start feeling blue, for no reason, and it turns out that Rosa is upset about something."

Neither Donna nor Kesha looked convinced. "Coincidence," Kesha stated. "Or maybe you could tell from looking at her that she was sad, so you started to feel sad because you care about her."

Martina shook her head. "No, it's more than that," she insisted. "Just last month, at school, I got a nosebleed, totally out of nowhere. Later, I found out that Rosa got hit in the face with a softball, and her nose started bleeding." She continued rapidly, before either of them could present an alternative explanation. "You see, sometimes it's like we're each one half of the same person. Honestly, I'm not saying it's ESP, but I swear, we can feel what each other is feeling." She could hear her own voice rising in intensity. "That's why I don't believe we're the only people on earth. Because I can feel her. She's not dead."

Donna and Kesha looked at each other, and Martina could read their reactions easily. Disbelief, then embarrassment, and then pity.

"She's not dead," she said again. "She's alive. They could all be alive."

"Then where are they, Martina?" Donna asked in a gentle voice, as if speaking to an obstinate child.

She felt like an idiot, but she couldn't stop now. "I don't know. Invisible, maybe. Or someplace else. But not dead. They're not dead." After a second, she added, "Maybe."

Donna took her hand. "I understand how you feel, Martina. I think about my older sister, and my little nephew. He was only six months old. I could cry and cry, just thinking about him. But we have to get on with our lives."

"You're in denial," Kesha declared to Martina. "You don't want to deal with the truth."

Donna grimaced. "Good grief, Kesha, show a little compassion."

Kesha glared right back at her. "Do you think I like saying this? Don't you think I miss my mother, my brothers, my grandparents? We've all lost people. But it's not good brooding about it. We have to face reality."

"It's not reality," Martina said. "We don't know what's going on, we don't know what happened.

Reality could be anything. Or nothing." Even as the words left her lips, she could hear how inane they sounded. And she couldn't believe how she was exposing her innermost thoughts to people she barely knew. This was a new experience for her. She'd always had Rosa to talk to.

But now Donna was distracted by something. She wrinkled her nose. "What's that smell?"

They were standing by a meat market, and the door was open. "Spoiled meat," Martina said. "We should have put it all in freezers last week."

The smell had hit Kesha now, and she made a face. "It's too late now. Besides, we're better off becoming vegetarians."

At that moment, three boys came out of the store. Each was carrying a big chunk of rancid beef. The smell made all three girls step back, and Donna was aghast. "You're not going to eat that, are you?"

One of the boys laughed. "Nah, we're gonna have some fun. Watch this." The three boys began whistling loudly, piercing the air with sharp, shrill noises.

"What are you doing?" Martina asked in bewilderment. Her question was answered in seconds. From an alley close by, a pack of growling dogs emerged, and raced toward the boys. Donna let out a shriek, grabbed Kesha and pulled her back into the doorway of a shop. But the dogs weren't interested in attacking the girls. They watched in horror as the creatures leaped for the hunks of meat that the boys were now tossing in the air and catching. The howls of the dogs blended with the boys' manic laughter. The boys tossed the meat higher and farther, while the dogs yelped frantically in their efforts to get it.

Martina moved back to the relative safety of the store entranceway. "Why are they doing that to those poor dogs? It's sickening!"

"They think they're having fun," Kesha said flatly.

"I had no idea there could be so many wild dogs in Manhattan," Donna whispered.

"They're not wild dogs," Kesha said. "Look at them. That's a poodle over there, and there are a couple of cocker spaniels. Most of them are wearing identification collars. They're pets. At least, they used to be pets."

Donna shuddered. "There must be animals like that all over the city. Scary."

"I think the guys are scarier," Martina commented. "Did you have to read *Lord of the Flies* in junior high? Given the right circumstances, ordinary kids can turn into savages."

"Don't get carried away," Kesha declared, but she was watching the carousing boys and frantic dogs uneasily.

"Let's get out of here," Donna said suddenly. "Let's go somewhere, do something."

"Like what?" Kesha asked.

"I don't know, something, anything. To get our minds off . . . everything." She turned to look at the shops that lined the avenue. "I know! Let's go Rollerblading."

"I don't know how to Rollerblade," Martina said.

"Have you ever been ice skating? Then you can Rollerblade. Come on, it'll be fun." Donna led the way to a nearby store that sold and rented Rollerblades.

It *was* like ice skating. Unfortunately, Martina had never been much of an ice skater. She managed to stay on her feet until they rounded a corner. Then her arms were flailing and she began to skid. Donna grabbed one of her arms, Kesha took the other, and Martina managed to pull them both down with her. No one was badly hurt as they collapsed in the road, and after the momentary shock, they all burst out laughing. Despite the pain in her rear end, Martina felt almost good. And after a few more falls, she began to get the hang of it. It was actually fun. Rosa would have liked this too.

"Let's head over to Fifth Avenue and go uptown," Kesha suggested. This was something they couldn't do if these were normal times—the traffic and crowds on the avenue would be prohibitive. Even now, they didn't have a clear path. Cars, buses, and trucks had to be circumvented, and on the sidewalks they had to maneuver around bikes and strollers. But every now and then there would be a clean stretch of road, and Martina felt like she was flying. She could feel the air move, blowing tension and fear out of her head. All she had to think about was staying on her feet.

They passed the Empire State Building and the New York Public Library. As they neared Saks Fifth Avenue, Donna slowed down to look in the windows.

"What do you think of that?" she asked, indicating a long dress in the window.

"Nice," Martina said, admiring the sleek sophistication of the elegant gown. "I wonder how much something like that costs."

"Two thousand, eight hundred and forty-five dollars," Donna told her.

"How did you know that?"

"My grandmother works at Saks." Donna corrected herself. "She worked at Saks. When I saw this dress in the window, I thought it would be perfect for the prom this spring. But even with Gramma's discount, it was too expensive."

"You could have it now," Martina said. "If you want it. You could just walk in the door, reach into the window and take it."

Donna shrugged. "It probably wouldn't even fit. My grandmother worked in designer dresses. Guess who one of her regular customers was? Travis's mother. It's weird when you think of it. While I was going out with Travis, she was unzipping his mother's dresses. We really lived in different worlds."

"Well, you're in the same world now," Kesha said flatly. "Come on, let's go." She took off, moving faster now. Donna and Martina followed her up Fifth Avenue, and they didn't pause again until they reached 59th Street. Kesha stopped there in the middle of the road, facing the Plaza Hotel.

"Have you ever been in there?" she asked the others.

Martina and Donna shook their heads.

"It's supposed to be really fancy," Kesha said. "Celebrities stay there."

"We could too, if we wanted to," Martina said.

"What's the point?" Kesha asked. "It's not like we could call room service." She took off to the east, and Martina and Donna followed. They were all moving slower now, and Martina thought the air felt heavier. She motioned to Donna to catch up with Kesha, and once they were together, she made them stop.

"I've got an idea," she said. "Bloomingdale's is right around the corner. Let's do makeovers."

"Makeovers? You mean, like with cosmetics?" Kesha's brow furrowed. "Why?"

Martina grinned. "Why not? You got something else to do?"

They skated into the Lexington Avenue entrance of the massive department store, and rolled slowly through accessories. They passed glass cases displaying jewelry, displays of handbags and scarves, leather gloves, and finally reached the cosmetics section. It seemed to go on for miles, with counters for every brand imaginable. Martina paused, trying to decide where to go first.

"Ooh," Donna cried, pointing to a sign, "Look at the free cosmetic case you get with any Estée Lauder purchase." Then they all laughed, because, of course, everything was free. But the laughter was a little forced, because the joke was getting old now.

"Who's going to do these makeovers?" Kesha asked as they gathered at a counter.

"I am," Martina said. "Who wants to go first?" She waved her hand at a stool.

Donna sat down. "You know how to do this?"

"My mother has a full-service beauty salon on Staten Island," Martina told her. As she spoke, she realized she was using the present tense again, but she didn't bother to correct herself. "Rosa and I have been helping out since we were little, sweeping up hair and bringing people magazines while they sat under the dryer. It's amazing how much you can learn from just hanging around." She surveyed the array of cosmetics displayed on the counter and felt like a little kid in a candy store. Then she studied Donna's face.

"What kind of look do you want? Glamorous? Innocent? Natural?"

Donna was getting into the spirit. "Oh, let's go for all-out sexy."

Martina went to work, although it felt more like play. She selected the wildest colors, bright iridescent eye shadows, turquoise pencils, powders and shadings to bring out Donna's bone structure. Kesha watched in amazement as Martina turned sweet Donna into Donna the vamp. With a flourish, Martina completed the transformation with an application of hot pink lipstick.

"How do I look?" Donna asked Kesha.

"Like a slut," Kesha replied. "Or a porno star."

"Cool!" Donna admired herself in the mirror. "You'd better not let Maura Kelly find out you can do this, Martina. She'll be begging for your services everyday."

"Me next, me next!" Kesha cried out.

Down-to-earth Kesha went for the exotic look, with thick black lines extending way beyond her eyes, and red lipstick so dark it was almost black. "You look like an Egyptian queen!" Donna cried out in delight.

Martina would have preferred to do her own makeup, but she allowed Kesha and Donna that privilege. She had a pretty good feeling she'd end up looking like a clown, but it was worth it for the sound of their laughter, which seemed to fill the empty store.

"Close your eyes," Kesha ordered, and Martina obliged. She could feel the brush passing over her eyelids, and she could tell by the pressure that Kesha was applying the shadow too thickly. She didn't care. With her eyes closed, she could pretend they weren't in this strange situation, a vacant department store, but back in her mother's Staten Island salon. How many times had she and Rosa given each other makeovers there? This was something she'd done a thousand times. But maybe that was why it was so much fun—it was ordinary good times, like the times she'd had before.

When they'd finished painting their faces, they sampled perfumes, and soon the air was nauseatingly sweet with the aroma of a hundred flowers. They escaped by way of the elevator, which took them up to lingerie. They looked over the lacy underwear and silky nightgowns, and then moved on to explore other floors. By the time they reached home furnishings, they were ready to collapse on the crushed velvet sofas.

"You know what's funny?" Donna mused. "I used to have a fantasy where I was locked in a department store overnight."

"What did you do?" Martina asked.

Donna smiled. "Exactly what we've been doing."

"So it's like we're living the fantasy," Kesha said.

"Or the nightmare."

Martina changed the subject quickly, before the conversation could take a depressing turn. "Are your feet hurting as much as mine are?"

"And we're going to have to skate back downtown," Donna said. "We left our shoes at the Rollerblade rental place, remember?"

"I don't think that's a problem," Martina replied. "Get back into the fantasy. Shoes are on five."

"Why do I feel like I'm shoplifting?" Kesha asked as she tried on some sturdy hiking boots. "It's not like I could actually buy these. There's no one to pay."

Donna was modeling a pair of spiked heels. "Gorgeous, aren't they?"

"Not very practical," Martina pointed out. "We've got fifty blocks to walk."

But as it turned out, they didn't walk all the way back to their hotel after all. They left Bloomingdale's on the Third Avenue side of the building, where Donna paused to stroke the hood of a shiny red Mustang convertible parked in front. "This is my fantasy car," she confessed to the others.

Martina peered through a window. "The keys are inside."

So Donna got to live another fantasy, though not for long. With all the vehicles on the streets, they soon reached a point where they were blocked from continuing. They had to abandon the Mustang, walk around the congestion, and take another car. This happened again and again, so by the time they reached Greenwich Village they were almost as tired as if they'd walked.

"There's a party going on," Kesha commented as they walked through the hotel lobby. They could hear music and voices, and it sounded like it was happening just above them.

"There's always a party going on," Martina said in an aggrieved tone. "I don't get it, they've got a whole city full of empty nightclubs and bars where they could be partying. Why do they have to do it here?"

She wasn't expecting a response and she didn't get one—but that might have been because of a scream that was shrill enough to be heard above the party noise. The girls ran up the stairs to the second floor, which already had a reputation as the party floor. Even so, they weren't prepared for the sight that presented itself.

It was like a replay of the scene in the school cafeteria on the first night, only worse. The whole floor looked like it had been totally trashed. There was junk all over the place, and the carpet bore evidence of food and cigarettes. Someone had thrown bottles against the walls, and dark wet stains had practically obliterated the pretty flowered wallpaper. Doors were covered with graffitti and a variety of dirty words. The party had obviously been going on for a week.

Loud music and raucous laughter poured out of several rooms. But then they heard another scream, and Maura Kelly came running out of a room.

Maura was a party girl, always had been. Frequently on Monday mornings, in the girls' restroom, Martina had heard her regaling anyone who would listen about the clubs she'd managed to talk her way into over the weekend, the bouncers she'd flirted with, what she had worn, who she had danced with.

She didn't look like she was in much of a party mood tonight. Her fists were clenched and she was pounding on Mike Salicki's chest. He was warding off her blows and laughing. "Hey, babe, you know you want it!"

"I do not want it and I particularly don't want it from you!" Maura shrieked. She tried to kick him in the groin but he managed to step aside in time. Now he was looking angry. He grabbed her arm.

"Look, bitch, it's going to happen sooner or later. We gotta reproduce, we have to repopulate the earth!"

As Maura struggled to break free of Mike, Kesha dashed forward and pushed him, catching him off guard. He stumbled and fell, and a stream of obscenities poured from his lips. By now, a couple of other kids had been drawn out into the hall by the noise. Some were laughing, others looked shocked.

Maura was crying now. Kesha put an arm around her. "C'mon, I'll walk you to your room. What floor are you on?" As they went down the hall, James DuPont sidled up alongside Martina.

"Wanna get naked?" he asked.

Martina glared at him, and then wrinkled her nose. "When was the last time you took a shower, James?"

He didn't take offense. "I'm going natural. Keeping it real, y'know? Feels good."

Martina took a step back. His smell was overpowering. It was affecting Donna too. "It's not so nice for everyone else, James," she admonished him.

"She's right," Martina said. "You keep this up, it could ruin your social life. Girls don't like boys who smell bad."

James sneered. "Girls can't be so picky anymore. Times have changed, Martina. Guys don't have to do anything we don't want to do anymore. And we can be anything we want to be. 'Cause you girls don't have much choice."

"You're disgusting," Donna declared. "Martina, let's get out of here." The two of them walked up two flights, to Donna's room. It was identical to Martina's.

"We should fix up these rooms," Martina said. "Put some art on the walls, get our own things. Personalize them. So we can feel more like we have homes."

Donna laughed, but there was no joy in it. "Some kids would be happier in caves."

"Like James?"

"And Mike. They're all turning into animals. And it's going to get worse."

Martina sank down on the bed. "Yeah, I know."

"I don't want to live like this," Donna said. She sat down next to Martina. "I guess I don't have any choice."

Martina shook her head. "We have a choice. We're human beings, we have to live like human beings."

"Maybe if we had a leader, a president," Donna suggested. "Someone who could get us organized, make us start planning for the future. At least, get people to feel like there is a future."

Martina considered this. "What about Kesha? She's got leadership qualities."

"No," Donna said. "Kesha's my best friend, but she's very opinionated, she's not very tactful, and she turns some people off. We need someone who's more generally popular. Someone with spirit."

Martina looked at her doubtfully. "Like a cheer-leader?"

"I was thinking of Travis. And that's not because I'm still torching for him," she added quickly. "But you have to admit, he can be charming. People trust him."

Martina wasn't so sure. "I haven't seen him around much this week. He's not showing what I'd call leadership qualities."

"I'm sure he's just as freaked out as the rest of us," Donna said. "Maybe he's afraid people expect him to do something, and he doesn't know what he should do. But if he knew we're concerned about what's going on, and that we'd help him out, he'd be willing to make some noise."

Personally, Martina had always thought Travis was sort of condescending, too much the typical phony smiling politico. But he'd won the class election by a landslide, and people did listen to him. At least he wasn't the type who would turn into a savage. She began to think that maybe talking to him wasn't such a bad idea. "Do you know where he's staying?"

"Top floor," Donna said quickly, and then she blushed. "No, I haven't been up there. I saw him on the elevator the other day and he pressed the penthouse button."

Martina had to smile. It figured that Travis would plant himself in the fanciest suite in the hotel. "Let's go see if he's there."

four

jake turned the corner at Bleecker Street and walked toward the Village Café. He used to pass this place all the time on his way home from school, and he was always attracted by what he saw through the big picture window. It was a quiet, slightly shabby place, where serious-looking types sat at small tables, writing on pads or typing on little portable PCs. One wall was lined with bookcases and magazine racks, and the magazines weren't the kind you found in your dentist's waiting room. They were literary magazines, poetry magazines, art magazines. Against the other long wall, there was a bar, but not the kind where fat, noisy men chugged beer and watched hockey on a big-screen TV. This bar served only coffee, but in a hundred different ways.

He'd never gone inside before. The place was too intimidating. The people inside looked like real writers, real poets, not high school kids with vague literary dreams. Surely, the men and women in the Village Café would spot him as an impostor.

There was no one to label him now. He strode into the café as if he belonged there. Dropping his jacket and his journal on a table by the big window, he went to the cappuccino machine behind the bar and fixed himself a coffee. He didn't add any foamy milk, though. The dates on the milk cartons had expired. Fresh milk had become a thing of the past by now.

It was nice outside, so he retrieved his things from the table and went to sit at one of the little terrace tables. It was unusually warm for an autumn day. Indian summer, this was called. Or was that a politically correct phrase anymore? Should he be thinking Native American summer?

He smiled at the way his mind was wandering, just as it used to when he sat through boring classes. An almost forgotten sense of well-being came over him. He opened his journal, and took a look at his last entry, dated almost two weeks ago.

> I still think Travis is a pompous, bureaucratic ass, but I have to admit, the ass can talk. I laughed when he put up notices demanding a meeting of the entire "community" (his word, not mine). But somehow he managed to get almost everyone together. He gave a corny pep talk, about making a new world, how we need to look out for each other if we want to survive, how we have to be a family and think of ourselves as brothers and sisters. He must have used every cliché in the book. But I guess it's what people wanted to hear, because they actually applauded him.

Two weeks after that meeting, Jake had to admit that Travis was more than just a good talker. He'd actually managed to get some things happening. Washington Square Park was being turned into a massive vegetable garden, and plans were being made to bring in fruit from orchards outside the city.

Some rules were set down too, about conserving energy and keeping the noise level in the hotel down. The party animals, like David and Maura, had moved their fiestas into bars and clubs around the city, music lovers were taking advantage of the fantastic sound systems available in concert halls and discos. Jocks had discovered indoor basketball courts, and they'd actually organized teams.

Now Travis was strutting around like he was Big Man on Campus again, still president of a somewhat-reduced senior class. He was even trying to start up some traditional high school activities again. He'd asked Jake and Martina to organize a community newspaper, and they'd agreed, assuming they could come up with something to report. He appointed a social committee to organize a senior prom in the spring. Pretty idiotic, Jake thought, considering the situation, but apparently some kids needed those things. There were still a lot of real problems they needed to confront, like the garbage and the packs of dogs that wandered the streets. But things had improved, people were acting less like animals, they were making routines for themselves, and life had become—well, livable.

For Jake, life wasn't bad at all. He had his own schedule, and it suited him nicely—in truth, it suited him better than the routine he'd had before. He spent his mornings here, at the Village Café, writing. At lunchtime, he'd gotten into the habit of meeting some others, Martina, Kesha, Donna, and sometimes Cam, for lunch. There was no more fresh food, but Donna was particularly good at thinking up new ways to put the contents of a can on top of pasta.

In the afternoons, he took a jog across the Brooklyn Bridge and back. Sometimes he went to a bookstore, or to a library. Or an art museum—he'd always been interested in art, but he'd never had much opportunity to explore it. Then he went over to the Art College, where he'd discovered fully equipped studios and art instruction videos. Now he could fool around with paints and canvases, without any teachers or fellow students looking over his shoulder.

For dinner, a lot of kids were now picking up frozen foods at a supermarket and then meeting in Domino's, a restaurant near the hotel, to eat them. Domino's was the sort of fancy, expensive place that no one other than Travis had ever eaten in before. Of course, it wasn't as if they could partake of the cuisine that was once served there, but there was something about the environment that made eating microwaved enchiladas more palatable.

The social committee had organized several events in the evenings—bowling, pool, ice skating. Sometimes he'd watch videos on the VCR in his room, or he'd watch them with others in the hotel lounge.

It was weird, in a way—Jake had always classified himself as a loner. He never hung out with a particular clique or gang, he wasn't a member of any teams, he didn't even like having a lab partner in biology. He rarely saw anyone from Madison outside of classes, and he usually brought a book to the school cafeteria at lunchtime to discourage anyone from joining him. Now, it would be even easier for him to continue as a loner, and instead he found himself willingly connecting with other people. There had to be some profoundly interesting psychological reason for this, but he didn't feel much like contemplating it. The day was too nice to think about problems that didn't have to be confronted.

He'd become good at not thinking about some things. Like his parents, home, the grandfather he'd adored. If he could go on blocking certain thoughts, he could get used to living like this.

In the silence of the city, his hearing had become more acute, and he knew someone was coming even before he saw Kesha appear at the corner. She strode toward him purposefully, and as she drew closer he saw a set look in her eyes that he'd come to recognize.

"What's up?" he asked as she sat down across from him.

"I had an idea," she said. "You know St. Anthony's?"

"The church?"

"No, the hospital. Medical Center, actually. My cousin Billy worked there, in an underground research laboratory. Something to do with radioactive isotopes."

"Okay," Jake said. "So?"

"Well, *we* survived because we were in that bomb shelter. Maybe they survived."

"Maybe who survived?"

"The people who worked in the underground laboratory. I once asked him if it was dangerous, working with radioactive material. He said they took a lot of precautions, and that the lab was the safest place on earth. An atom bomb couldn't touch them. What do you think?"

"First of all," Jake began, "we don't know why we survived. I don't think it's because we were in a bomb shelter. I mean, there were other places like that. If everyone working underground survived, where are they now? Still hanging out underground?"

"Maybe," Kesha said. "Or they could be anywhere. This is a big city, Jake. We've been pretty much sticking to this area. There could be people sitting in a café on the Upper West Side, and we wouldn't know about them."

He hated to pour cold water on her hopes, but she'd have to face reality sooner or later. "Kesha . . . remember what Travis said the other night? About accepting the situation and getting on with our lives?"

Kesha's eyes went cold. "Thanks, but I don't need any advice from Travis Darrow. I can't believe you bought into his stupid lecture. Didn't it sound like a campaign speech to you?"

This was true, but everything Travis said sounded like a politician's babble. "You're just holding a grudge. You're going to find something wrong with everything he says or does. Give it up, Kesha. That class election was ages ago, in another world."

"It's not that," Kesha insisted. "There's something about his attitude. I don't trust him. He's not the kind of person who does anything out of the goodness of his heart. He's got to have ulterior motives."

"Like what?" Jake asked. "You think he wants to be voted 'most likely to succeed' so he can have a big photo in the yearbook? I got news for you,

Kesha. There isn't going to be any yearbook this year."

"It doesn't matter," Kesha said impatiently. "I'm just saying I think we should check out all possibilities before we write off humanity."

He could see she wasn't going to give up easily. "Where is this St. Anthony's Medical Center?"

"On the east side, in the thirties. I'm going over there now."

Three weeks of knowing Kesha had taught him not to expect her to actually ask for a favor. "You want me to come with you?"

"If you want."

"Okay," Jake said. "But I want to stop at the hotel and drop off my jacket."

They were walking through the lobby when the elevator doors opened and Ashley stepped out. Her head was down and she passed Jake and Kesha without acknowledging them.

"You ever talk to her?" Jake asked Kesha.

"Who, the supermodel? Why would I talk to her? She's never said a word to me. Or anyone I know, for that matter."

"She looks depressed," Jake commented.

"Nah, that's the high fashion style. Models always look bored." She shot him a curious look. "Don't tell me you're interested in her."

He grinned. "What if I am?"

"No offense, Robbins, but she's out of your league."

Just a few weeks ago, he would have agreed with her. But weren't they all in the same league now?

St. Anthony's Medical Center was a massive establishment, comprised of several buildings and encompassing two city blocks. Kesha had no idea where her cousin's laboratory was, so they spent almost an hour wandering from building to building, looking for a directory. When they were finally able to locate the right building, they had to descend three flights into a subterranean area behind a heavy metal door.

It was dark and silent in the windowless hall. No—it wasn't completely silent. From somewhere came a whirring sound. They went in that direction.

They walked quickly, checking the names on the doors they passed. Jake felt removed from the world, just as he used to feel in his geometry class at Madison. Despite himself, he could feel his pulse quickening. Someone could survive a bomb down here.

The whirring became louder. They reached the very end of the hall and a door with a sign on it: ISOTOPE LABORATORY. "Maybe we should put something over our faces," Jake suggested, but Kesha ignored him. She turned the knob and walked in.

The room was empty. The whirring sound came from an air-circulating fan.

Kesha backed out and closed the door. Silently, they went back up to the main floor and left the building.

"I'm sorry," Jake said. "Were you close to your cousin?"

"No, not particularly." Kesha frowned. "It just doesn't make sense. The people who were in that room should be alive. Why us and not them?"

"Even if they did survive, I seriously doubt that they'd be hanging around here," Jake said.

"So where are they?"

"Kesha, weren't you the one who said there's no

point in asking questions that can't be answered?"

"Yeah." Kesha sighed. "I hate agreeing with Travis."

"Don't worry," Jake assured her. "I'm sure he'll come up with an idea or two you won't like."

But the idea Travis presented to Jake later that day wasn't bad at all. He cornered Jake over dinner. "I need your help," he said, taking a seat at the table. Travis was the kind of person who always assumed he'd be welcome anywhere he went. The fact that Kesha was at the table and glaring in his direction didn't seem to bother him at all.

"There are kids around who seem really depressed," Travis continued.

Martina looked up from her Lean Cuisine. "Does that surprise you, Travis?"

Travis smiled. "I know what you're saying, Martina. No one's jumping for joy. But most of us are starting to cope and deal with things. On the other hand, some kids are still acting like zombies, like they're on the brink of suicide."

"Jessica Mendez," Donna proposed. "She's always crying. And Alex Popov. I don't think he's physically capable of smiling."

Kesha shrugged. "He never smiled before all this happened, I don't know why he'd start smiling now."

"Shalini," Martina suggested.

"Who?" Travis asked.

"The little Indian girl. The one who no one ever notices."

"Oh right, of course, Shalini." It was clear that he had no idea who Martina was talking about. He turned back to Jake. "Anyway, I was thinking, maybe you could organize some sort of therapy group to help them."

"Why me?" Jake asked. "I'm not a psychologist."

"You know that creative writing class we had together last year? You wrote a poem, about people tuning in to other people's feelings without intruding on them."

Despite himself, Jake was flattered. "You remember my poem?"

"Yes, it made a lasting impression on me," Travis said with a little more sincerity than was absolutely necessary. "I thought it was really sensitive. Maybe you could get these depressed people to talk about their feelings, find something to be interested in. How about it?"

"Let me think about it," Jake said. "I'll get back to you."

"Great," Travis said warmly. He saluted the others at the table and left.

Donna gazed after him. "That was nice. He really cares about those people."

Kesha snorted. "Oh, please. They're not people, they're votes."

"Are you going to do it?" Martina asked Jake.

"I don't know." Jake had never seen himself as the kind of person other people would want to confide in. When he'd written that poem last year, he'd been talking about recognizing feelings, not sharing them. Travis wasn't capable of picking up on a subtle difference like that.

But then he thought about one truly depressed person he'd noticed. Ashley Silver . . . this would give him an excuse to approach her. Get to know her. Find out if current circumstances really did put them in the same league now.

There had to be some benefits to being the only people on earth.

martina was grateful for the Internet. Nothing new was being added, of course, but there were still a zillion Web sites she could explore. Now that she could have a state-of-the-art computer with full color and a big screen, she could really appreciate them. Surfing the net made her feel like there was still a world out there.

But on that morning, her computer gave her a shock. She had just accessed her server when an icon she hadn't seen for a long time appeared on the screen. It was the little flag telling her that she had mail. She clicked on it.

For a moment she just sat there and stared at the name that followed the word "From." Rosa. Rosa had sent her a message.

Her hand trembled as she clicked to open the message.

I'm sitting in the computer lab, and I'm seriously bored. Have you seen Angela Kingston? She's sitting right in front of me. She's got a blue streak in her hair; it looks really stupid.

That was it. The message had been written more than three weeks ago. It had just been delayed.

She didn't know whether to laugh at herself or burst into tears. Had she really thought Rosa was reaching out to her from wherever she was? A voice from beyond the grave?

No, not the grave. She couldn't accept that. She'd been trying to cope, trying not to brood, but with this late message, the feelings came rushing back. Still, she didn't burst into tears. Instead, she shut down the computer and left the room.

Indian summer had been brief. The skies were cloudy that day, and Martina shivered slightly when she went outside. She needed to go to a store and pick out a warmer coat, but not now. Besides, maybe the shiver wasn't actually a response to the weather. It wasn't really all that cold.

She crossed the street, zigzagging around the cars that had become permanent fixtures in the road. The rhythm of her heartbeat picked up as she approached Madison High. She went directly to the main entrance.

Inside, the silence seemed even eerier than it did outside. She could hear her footsteps, even though she was wearing soft-soled tennis shoes. Afraid she might lose her nerve, she practically ran up the stairs to the second floor.

She knew which classroom Rosa had been in during fifth period. When she arrived at the door, she opened it slowly, as if unsure of what she might find on the other side.

There were no surprises. What she saw was a typical class—European history, from the look of the blackboard. It displayed a chronology of British monarchs, up to Elizabeth I. Apparently, the teacher had been interrupted in the middle of that last entry, since it only read *Eliza*. On the desks were open notebooks, pens and pencils, textbooks. Hanging from the backs of chairs were sweaters and jackets. Bags and backpacks littered the floor. There was nothing unusual about the sight. Only the people were missing.

Martina walked up and down the rows until she spotted Rosa's plastic folder on a desk. She sat down there.

She had come in search of something, anything, that had belonged to her sister. Her bag, a book, a sweater . . . something that would serve as a souvenir, a remembrance. But as she leaned back in Rosa's chair, staring at the incomplete chronology on the blackboard—perhaps the last sight Rosa had seen—she understood that what she really wanted was something else.

If it was true that identical twins were capable of some sort of extrasensory perception, she wanted evidence of that now. She didn't expect to see Rosa, or hear her. But she wanted to feel her, to have an awareness that somewhere, somehow, she existed. Closing her eyes, she conjured up an image of Rosa and concentrated with all her might on establishing a connection. Nothing happened.

She opened her eyes and gazed around the room. She spotted a metal object on a nearby desk. A Walkman? She got up to look. No, it was a miniature tape recorder. She recalled Rosa telling her about a girl in her class who had a hearing impairment, and taped all the lectures so that she could listen to them again at a higher volume. Martina examined the machine. She hit REWIND, let it run for a few seconds, and then pressed PLAY.

She jumped at the sound of the teacher's voice. It was very clear, as if the teacher were right there in the room talking. "With his first wife, Catherine of Aragon, Henry VIII had one child, Mary. When he decided to divorce his wife in order to marry Anne Boleyn, he assumed that Anne Boleyn would produce a male heir, so he declared that—" The next sound was a gasp, a sharp intake of breath. This was followed by a faint shriek, and a jumble of unintelligible words and sounds. Then there was silence. And the tape remained silent until it ran out.

She rewound the tape and listened again. And again, and again. By the fourth time, she thought she was able to make out some of the expressions before the silence. There were a couple of expletives, and then something that sounded like "what mumble mumble." What's happening? What's going on?

She searched through the knapsack that rested by the desk where she'd found the recorder. In it, she found an earphone. She attached it, put the phone in her ear, rewound the tape, and turned up the volume. It was still a jumble of garbled sounds, and there was static too, but she could almost swear she heard someone say, "What do you want?"

"What do you want?" Who was the person speaking to? Had there been an intruder in the classroom? She was about to rewind the tape for another listening when she heard a noise.

She froze. It was a creak, the sound of a footstep on a weak floorboard, and it came from out in the hall. Holding her breath, she rose gingerly, trying not to let her chair squeak. She tiptoed to the doorway and looked around the edge of the doorframe.

Her breath came out in a rush. "Cam! What are you doing here?"

Cameron Daley was as startled as she was. "I could ask you the same thing," he said.

Martina hesitated. She'd known Cam since freshman year, and they'd once worked together on a sociology project, but she didn't know him well. He was a quiet guy, sort of nerdy.

"I was in my sister's fifth period classroom," she told him. "The class she was in when, you know . . ."

Cam nodded. "I was down in the chemistry lab. I found this." He indicated the metal object he was holding.

"What is it?"

"An old Geiger counter. It can detect levels of radiation in the atmosphere."

"Oh."

"Everyone seems to be assuming that there's been some sort of nuclear bomb explosion. I want to see if that's true."

"Can you tell, three weeks later?"

"Sure. The radiation from a nuclear blast can remain in the atmosphere for hundreds of years." He nodded toward the stairs leading to the exit. "Want to come with me?"

"Okay." They went downstairs and outside. Cam fiddled with the machine, and then studied it for a few minutes. He went out into the street, still watching the machine. Then he returned.

"Nothing," he said.

"No radiation?" She looked at the machine. "Maybe it's not working."

He shook his head. "I tested it on a piece of radium in the chemistry lab. It works fine."

"Then there wasn't any bomb."

"Doesn't seem like it."

The unspoken question hung in the air.

"Come with me," Martina said suddenly. "I want you to hear something." He followed her back to Rosa's classroom.

"Listen to this." She rewound the tape and gave him the earphone. He listened intently.

"What did you hear?" she asked him when he removed the earphone.

"I'm not sure," he said. "Someone screams, someone yells 'ohmigod.' Then 'what do something something.' "

"Listen again," she urged. He did.

"Well?" she asked when he finished.

"What do . . ." He paused.

" 'What do you want?' "

"Maybe."

She met his eyes urgently. "Like, maybe, somebody was there? Someone who wasn't supposed to be there?"

"Maybe," he said again. He didn't look convinced. But he did look intrigued.

Alex studied the notice taped to the wall just outside his hotel room: *Anyone interested in forming a bowling league, meet tonight in lobby, 7:00.*

"You into bowling, Popov?"

Alex gave Carlos Guzman a withering look, and shook his head briefly.

"You ever tried it?" Carlos asked. "We had a good time bowling the other day. Want to join us tonight?"

"No." He went back into his room and shut the door. If he wasn't interested in hanging out with those morons when life was normal, why would he be interested now?

He fell back on the bed and stared up at the ceiling. What was he going to do tonight? He could pick up some videos and watch them on the brand new VCR he'd just installed. That had been a hoot, marching into Radio Shack and picking out whatever caught his eye. Maybe he should go back there and check out the giant screen TVs. Though it might not be easy fitting something that big into this little room. It was stupid, when he thought about it. What was he doing in this rinky-dink hotel room when there was a whole city of apartments to choose from? He could have one of those massive Tribeca lofts if he wanted one. He could toss out the crap that had belonged to the poor slobs who'd been living there, and fix it up his own way. He could grab the biggest Harley he could find, cruise the city, pick up some CDs. Maybe he should find himself a guitar and one of those teach-yourself books. There were a lot of things he could do.

But he continued to lie flat on his back and look at the ceiling. Actually, this could be the best thing to do—absolutely nothing. He liked being alone, no one ordering him around, no one making any demands on him. No errands to run for his nagging, whining mother. No brother sending him out to score some coke. No drunken stepfather dropping by to smack him around. Peace. It was wonderful. And eventually, the other survivors would give up trying to get him involved in things.

Because he wasn't interested, not in anything they had to propose. He wasn't up for constructing a new society. He didn't want to party with the ones who thought they were all on the brink of extinction. Those first few days, when everyone walked around like zombies, in a state of shock, were easier. Now that most of his classmates were reverting to their original personalities, this place had become almost as annoying as Madison High. He really should start thinking about getting out of here.

There was a knock on the door. Alex ignored it, but the knocking continued. He sat up. "Yeah, what?"

The door opened. A guy stood there. "Hi."

Alex just stared at him without speaking.

"I'm Jake Robbins. From geometry class."

"No kidding," Alex muttered. "I thought you were my next door neighbor from Brighton Beach."

Jake didn't react to the sarcasm. "I was talking to Travis, about getting a group together to—"

Alex didn't let him finish. "I'm not interested in any groups."

"I haven't even told you what it's about."

"It doesn't matter," Alex said. "I'm not interested."

"Yeah, well . . . if you change your mind—"

"I won't."

Jake backed out, and Alex sank back down on the bed. Now they were going to start bugging him in his own room. He really had to get out of here. Maybe he wasn't ready to start looking for a new residence, but he could get himself out for the evening.

He could go to the movies, the real movies. He used to get so irritated in movie theaters, with people talking and babies crying and the smell of popcorn, which made him nauseous. He fantasized about sitting alone in a theater, enjoying the big screen with no interruptions. It couldn't be too hard to run a movie reel on a projector.

The Angelika on Houston had six screens. There had to be something over there he could stand watching.

He managed to get out of the hotel without running into any more friendly classmates. Walking rapidly in the chilly night air, he hugged his battered old leather jacket tighter. That was something he could do tomorrow—check out some stores for a warmer leather jacket. That should kill a couple of hours.

The films advertised outside the Angelika didn't grab him. There were a couple of foreign films with subtitles, a documentary about whales, and another about transvestite steelworkers. He settled on a comedy that had something to do with alien abductions, and went inside.

He wandered around, searching for projection booths. He found the one that contained the alien abduction film, and set it up on the projector. Then he went out into the seating area and sat down.

Nothing happened. He must have put the film on wrong. He got up, and then he thought he heard something. He looked hard at the screen, but it was still black. Then he realized the noise was coming from the other side of the room.

Rats? The idea made him feel queasy. But after a few moments he was able to identify the sound. Someone was crying.

His first impulse was to get out of there. The last thing he wanted was a run-in with some thoroughly depressed kid who wanted to talk. But as his eyes adjusted to the dark of the theater, he saw the girl, huddled in a seat, looking totally pathetic. She was from his geometry class, of course, but he didn't know her name.

He edged over toward her. At the sound of his

footsteps, she caught her breath and turned toward him. There was fear on her face.

"You okay?" he asked.

"Yes," she whispered. "I'm sorry."

"Sorry for what?"

"I am sorry to have disturbed you."

It was the first time he'd ever heard an apology like that. He didn't know how to react. "S'okay," he mumbled. "See ya."

He started up the aisle. She turned away from him and buried her face in her arms again. He wanted to get out of there, but he kept looking at her. Reluctantly, he went back.

"Uh, you sure you're okay?"

She kept her face in her arms, but he could hear her muffled "yes."

"Then why are you crying?"

She lifted her head and turned back to him. Her eyes were wide. "Are you not feeling sad?"

He thought everyone had recovered from the first shock by now. Apparently not.

"I guess you miss your family," he said uncomfortably.

"Don't you?"

He shrugged. "We weren't all that close."

She looked perplexed, as if he was speaking a foreign language. "You were not close to your mother and father?"

"No. Were you?"

"Yes," she said. "Indian families are very close."

He could have told her that Russian families normally were close, too, just not in his case. "Were you born in India?"

"No, but my parents came here just before I was born."

He was mildly surprised to hear that. She had

a foreign look, and the stiff way she spoke wasn't very American.

"Were you born here?" she asked.

"I was born in Russia," he told her. "Actually, it was the Soviet Union then." Impulsively, he asked, "Were your parents more Indian than American?"

"Oh, yes," she said. "My mother wears a sari. And my father is very traditional. He arranged a marriage for me when I was born."

"You're kidding!" Alex exclaimed. He didn't know that kind of thing still went on anymore. Despite himself, he was intrigued. "You already know who you're going to marry? I hope for your sake it's someone you like."

"I have never met him," she said simply. "His name is Ahmed, and he lives in Calcutta. He will come to New York in June and we will marry after graduation."

This was too weird for him. His expression must have given this away because she explained, "This is common among people of our kind."

"Do you *want* to marry this guy?" He realized he was speaking in the present tense, just as she was.

"It is not my decision," she said.

"Are you nuts?" he asked bluntly.

She looked at him questioningly.

"Are you saying you're going to marry someone just because your father tells you to?"

She still didn't respond.

He laughed shortly. "Well, I guess it doesn't matter now."

"What do you mean?" she asked.

"This guy, Ahmed—he's not around anymore. Neither is your father."

He was alarmed to see her eyes fill with tears again. "Hey, take it easy," he said. "I'm not telling you anything you don't already now."

"I am so frightened," she whispered. "I am alone now."

"Yeah, well, we're all alone," he muttered. He wasn't sure if he heard her, and he decided not to repeat this. She was so small, she looked so fragile . . . Alex was feeling bigger and stronger than he really was.

"Look, it'll be okay," he said gruffly. "We'll survive."

She looked up at him with those big brown eyes. Was it his imagination, or was there awe in those eyes? He had an almost overwhelming urge to put an arm around her. "You want to go for a walk?" he asked.

Her eyes widened. She still looked frightened. But she stood up, and she said "yes."

"**what do you** think?" Jake asked Martina and Kesha. They were looking over the first issue of the *New World*, hot off the press.

"It's okay," Martina said. "Like a real newspaper. Only smaller."

"Twenty-five people can't make that much news," Jake reminded her. "I'm surprised we were able to fill both sides of one sheet. Even using the largest typeface."

The headline announced the formation of two mixed-sex basketball teams, and the article raised the question of which rules would be followed, men's or women's. Another article described the facilities available at nearby health clubs. There was a report on the ongoing efforts to bury rotten food, and a letter to the editor, suggesting that plans be made for trips outside the city to seek out animals for food.

"That's stupid," Kesha fumed. "We're better off becoming vegetarians." She turned the sheet over and groaned. "I hope this isn't going to be a regular feature," she said, pointing to the piece entitled "Viewpoint" with the byline Travis Darrow.

Martina read it out loud. "Unity—this must be

our guiding word. We are all individuals, and we each have our own attitudes, tastes, politics, religious beliefs, and styles. But there is something that we share, something which links us. And I'm not talking about Madison High school spirit. We share the desire to survive. Not only to survive, but to endure. Whatever happened to our families, our friends, our loved ones, all the other people in the world—we can't do anything about that. But we can keep their world, our world, alive. We can keep this world moving and growing. We have to be our own family now, to think of ourselves as brothers and sisters, and to live together in peace."

Kesha made a gagging noise. "I don't think Travis Darrow has had an original or creative thought in his life."

Jake grinned. "Yeah, okay, but at least his intentions are good. Look, if you guys have any bright ideas, write them up so we can come out with another issue next week."

Martina was on the verge of telling him she might have a headline for the next issue, but then she thought better of it. So far, she hadn't told anyone about the tape she'd found in her sister's classroom. Only Cam knew, and she'd sworn him to silence. She needed to feel more certain about what she had heard before people got too excited. She was planning to go to an electronics store today, and get the highest quality tape player she could find.

The only problem was, she knew nothing about tape players, and she had no idea what she'd be looking for. She looked around for Cam that morning, but he was notorious for spending his days in bookstores, and there were only about a zillion bookstores in New York. There was no way of knowing which one he was visiting today.

When she met Donna in the lobby for lunch, she asked her if she knew anything about tape players. "Like, do you have any idea which brand is best?"

"How do you mean, the best?"

"I have this tape I want to listen to, and, and I want to make sure I'm hearing everything right." She knew her explanation sounded lame, but Donna got the point. Her brow furrowed.

"Let me think . . ." Then she brightened. "Let's ask Travis."

"Why Travis?"

"He's very into that stuff. When I was going out with him, he was looking for a new tape deck for his car, and he used to go on and on, comparing one brand to another. I know where he is, too. I just saw him going into that photocopy store down the street."

Martina allowed herself to be dragged down the street, knowing full well that Donna was mainly looking for an excuse to talk to Travis. But when Travis asked her what kind of tape it was, she decided he'd be a good person to explain it all to. He wasn't the type to blow it out of proportion.

She explained to him how she'd found the tape, and what she thought she'd heard. "There's no explosion or anything like that. And the way people are yelling, it doesn't sound like a reaction to a bomb. It's more like they're seeing something they didn't expect to see. Something or . . . someone."

Travis gave her a patronizing smile. "Oh, Martina, come on. Are you sure about that?"

"No," Martina said promptly. "I'm not sure.

That's why I want to listen to the tape on a high quality player."

"Do you have it with you?" he asked.

She took it out of her bag. "Yeah, but I don't have a player."

"I've got a good system in my room," he told her. "How about letting me take this and listen to it when I have a chance?"

"Yeah, I guess that would be okay," Martina agreed.

"I'd like to hear it too," Donna said.

Either Travis didn't pick up on the hint or he chose to ignore it. "Martina, have you let anyone else hear this?"

"Just Cam. I saw him at school when I found it."

"Well, I think you might not want to mention it in front of anyone else. We don't want people to freak out. Or get any false hopes."

Personally, Martina thought that false hopes were better than no hopes, but she could see Travis's point. "Okay. Let me know what you think after you listen to the tape."

"Absolutely," Travis promised.

"Come on, Donna." She was about to leave when Travis said, "Oh, Martina, by the way . . . you said you found this at school?"

She nodded. "In my sister's classroom."

Travis frowned slightly, looking for all the world like someone's mildly disapproving father. "Martina, I don't think it's a good idea for you to go off exploring like that, on your own, without anyone knowing where you are."

"Why not? You think whatever happened to everyone else could happen to me? Travis, it didn't just happen at school. Everyone who was in this hotel at that time disappeared too."

"I think I know what Travis means," Donna piped up eagerly. "What if you had fallen down the stairs and banged your head? What if you were unconscious? Nobody would know where to look for you."

"Exactly," Travis said, and gave Donna a brief smile of approval. Martina thought the girl would pass out from joy. "I'm just telling you this for your own good, Martina. We wouldn't want anything to happen to you. So be careful, okay?"

"Oh, I will," Martina said solemnly. She would be very careful not to tell Travis about anything she did. She'd never liked it when her own father scolded her. Surely she shouldn't have to put up with patronizing lectures from Travis Darrow.

Jake was getting ready to meet with his depression group. He'd posted signs on every hall in the hotel, and he thought he'd come up with a good approach. The meeting was to be held at a health club, across the street. From his own experience, he knew that physical exercise was good for depression. Besides, the camaraderie that could result from working out together might help people open up and talk.

He had no idea how many of his classmates to expect. Everyone here had to be experiencing something. Some of them had recovered from the initial shock, but there had to be a lot of lingering sadness and fear. He had a feeling most of the guys wouldn't want to admit this, but if at least a couple of them showed up, the word would get around that this wasn't an uncool thing to do. As for the girls . . . it might be easier for them to admit to their feelings. He hoped it would be easy for one in particular.

Mentally, he practiced his opening remarks as he walked to the health club. He needed to gain their trust, and he didn't want to scare them away. He wanted to come across as low key, and sincere. Friendly, but not pushy. This was new territory for him. Mister Independent, Mister Keep-Your-Distance, posing as someone people could confide in. What a guy would go through to meet a girl . . .

At the health club, he went upstairs to the equipment room, where the signs had instructed them to meet. He figured that if people were occupied, if they had something to concentrate on, it would relax them. At least they wouldn't have to look directly at each other. Or at him. The thought of a dozen pair of eyes aimed in his direction gave him the creeps.

But when he walked into the room, he saw right away that he wasn't going to have to worry about this. The place was deserted. No, wait—there was someone sitting on the biceps extension machine. Someone with a cloud of soft light curls framing an exquisite face . . . How lucky could a person get? The only person who had showed up was the girl of his dreams.

"Hi."

She looked up. A drop of sweat was moving slowly down the side of her face. On her it looked good. "Hello."

"I'm, uh, glad you could come."

She looked a little puzzled.

"How are you feeling today?" he asked.

"Fine," she replied. But of course, people always said that, whether they were really fine or on the brink of throwing themselves off a cliff. And then she asked, "How are *you*?"

This was good, this was the perfect opening.

"Well," he said slowly, "that's not an easy question to answer anymore, is it? I mean, we're all struggling with this change in our lives, trying to figure out what happened, why we're here, where we're going. My feelings are so conflicted, just as yours are. Why do you think that is?"

She stared at him, her mouth slightly open.

"You look surprised at what I'm saying," he said.

"I am," she replied.

"Why?"

"Because—because I thought you'd just say 'fine.' I mean, that's what people usually say when you ask, 'How are you?' "

"Well, yeah, sure," he said, suddenly feeling tongue-tied. "But I figured, if you're here, you'd want to talk about feelings."

Now she looked completely bewildered. "Not really," she said.

"You're not depressed?"

"Sure I'm depressed. Isn't everybody? But that's not why I came here."

"Why did you come here?"

"To work out! Isn't that what a person usually goes to a health club for?"

Suddenly, he felt very, very small. "You didn't come here for the depression therapy group, did you?"

"No." Her expression became sympathetic. "Is that why you're here?"

"Oh, no," he said quickly. Then, "Well, yes, but not because I'm depressed or anything like that. I can handle what's going on. I was, um, just trying to organize a group, for, you know, people who, who wanted to talk . . ." He was stammering like an idiot.

"Why?"

"Because, because Travis asked me to, see, I wrote this poem and he thought I understood feelings, and I don't really, I mean, I care about feelings, but . . . well, I don't know, but anyway . . ." He gave up. "Never mind." He wanted to slink out of the room and disappear. Now he really was depressed.

Then she smiled, and he felt a hundred times better. "Why did you think I was particularly depressed?" she asked.

"Well, you were always by yourself, and you never seemed to be talking to anyone else."

"No one ever talks to me," she said. "Of course, very few people spoke to me before all this happened. I guess there's no reason for them to start talking to me now." She didn't sound bitter, just matter-of-fact.

"Maybe they were intimidated by you," Jake suggested. He knew that was true for him.

"I was just a model, for crying out loud. It's not like I was some sort of genius. I'm just a face and a body."

"Oh, I'm sure you're more than that," Jake said, even though her face and body seemed enough to him.

"Of course I'm more than that," Ashley snapped. "But that's what they saw. Of course, there were the ones like Maura Kelly, who talked to me all the time, because they thought I could get them into clubs or introduce them to movie stars. Now that there are no more movie stars, *they* don't even bother talking to me."

"Gee," Jake said. "That's rough. How did you get to be a model, anyway?" The moment the words left his lips, he realized how lame they sounded.

Now she would think he was just another star-struck moron who wanted to know what Brad Pitt was really like.

But she actually deigned to answer him. "I was discovered on a plane. My mom and I were going to visit my grandmother in California, and we got bumped up to first class. This modeling agent was sitting across the aisle from us, and she kept looking at me."

Jake wasn't surprised. "You're very beautiful," he blurted out.

She didn't bother to thank him. "I'm different looking," she admitted. "I can't take any credit for it, it's all in the genes. My father was the son of a German Jew and a Chinese woman. My mother was African-American. I just lucked out, I guess."

"You liked modeling?" Jake noticed that Ashley was actually using the past tense when she spoke about her family. In a way, she sounded healthier than the other kids.

"I liked the money," she said frankly. "And it wasn't exactly hard work. I mean, it could get boring, just standing there for hours. But it wasn't as if I had to lift bricks. Or even *think*."

"Do you miss it?"

"I miss a lot of things. Hey, what is this, an interrogation? How come you get to ask all the questions?"

He bowed his head humbly. "My life's kind of boring compared to yours." But he found himself telling her about his love for writing, his poetry and his unfinished novels and his dream of living in a Parisian garret and scribbling the great American novel. "I guess I can forget about that now," he added.

She shrugged. "Can you think of anything good about what's happened?"

He considered this. "Well, I don't have to break my parents' heart. They want, they wanted, me to be a lawyer or a doctor, not a starving artist type. What about you? Is anything better for you?"

She replied promptly. "Chocolate."

"Huh?"

"In case you never noticed, models have to be skinny. For some of them, it comes naturally. The rest of us live on carrot sticks and Diet Coke."

"Oh." After a moment, he asked, "You ever tried 'Heavenly Chunky Mudcake'?"

"What's that?"

"A new Ben and Jerry's flavor. Dark chocolate chunks, pecans, brownie bits and fudge streaks in mocha ice cream."

She gasped.

"I'm sure there's a carton left in a store around here. Wanna go look for one?"

"Now *that* sounds like a cure for depression," she said. She hopped off the machine.

Alex hugged the warm grocery bag close to himself as he walked into the hotel. There was no one in the lobby. Reassured that all was well, he got on the elevator.

"Hold the door!" someone yelled.

Alex automatically hit the CLOSE DOOR button but he wasn't fast enough. A couple of bozos in Madison High football jackets pushed their way through the closing doors. The red-haired one eyed Alex's bag.

"Whatcha got there?" he asked.

"Stuff," Alex mumbled, hoping the contents of his bag wouldn't give him away. He didn't like the way the two boys were grinning, so when the door opened on the next floor, he scooted out and headed toward the stairwell. He didn't know why he was being so mysterious—it wasn't like he was doing something illegal.

He'd walked Shalini home the night before, so he knew where her room was. He knocked on the door, and heard her timid voice asking, "Who is it?"

"Me. Alex."

She opened the door and eyed him nervously.

"I got something for you," he said. He brushed past her and went into the room. Then he put the bag on her bed. Shalini let out a little shriek as the bag began moving. Her shriek turned into a laugh as a little cocker spaniel puppy crawled out.

"He's so cute!" she cried out, and gathered the dog in her arms.

"You said you missed your dog," Alex said. "And I saw this one just around the corner."

"He's hungry," Shalini said as the puppy began licking her face.

"I picked up some dog food," Alex said. "It's in the bag."

Shalini's eyes were shining. "You brought him here for me?"

"Yeah, well, you were so down last night . . ."

He still wasn't quite sure why he'd knocked himself out looking for a cocker spaniel, just because that was the kind of dog she used to have. But he had to admit, he liked the way she was looking at him, with awe and adoration.

Shalini busied herself opening the can of dog food and putting the stuff on a plate. Overjoyed, the puppy began barking like a maniac. He tore into the food, and when he was finished, he started barking again.

"For a little guy he can really bark," Alex said.

Shalini nodded happily. "My spaniel was just like that." She spooned out some more food for him.

Just then, there was a banging on her door. "Who is it?" Alex yelled.

"I'm trying to sleep," someone yelled back. "Shut that damn dog up!"

"Go to hell!" Alex called out.

Shalini looked concerned. "Maybe I should move to another floor where I won't have neighbors. I don't think there's anyone up on five."

"You stay right here," Alex declared. "If that jerk doesn't like the noise, *he* can move."

Shalini looked at him doubtfully.

"Don't worry," Alex assured her. "I'm not going to let anyone mess with you."

And he was rewarded with another look of adoration.

seven

martina hadn't been in this particular bookstore since it had been turned into a so-called "superstore." Now she understood where that word came from. It was like one of those massive supermarkets, where you could never find something simple, like a can of green beans. She had absolutely no idea where to go to find what she wanted. She wasn't even sure *what* she wanted.

But luck was with her that day. In her fruitless wanderings, she somehow ended up in natural sciences, and there she found Cam. "Cam, thank goodness. Do you know where anything is in this place?"

"What are you looking for?"

"Is there a book or magazine that tells you what's the best kind of equipment?"

"There's *Consumer Reports*," Cam said.

"Isn't there something more specialized, about music equipment?"

"Does this have something to do with that tape you found?"

She'd been reluctant to talk about it. Every time she brought up the question of what happened, people ignored her or changed the subject. But

Cam hadn't laughed at her when she first showed him the tape, and he still looked interested now. "I thought that if I listened to it on some high quality machine I could hear more. I remember seeing this cop show once, where the detectives played an answering machine tape on high-tech equipment, and they could hear stuff going on in the background that they couldn't hear before."

Cam looked interested. "That's not a bad idea. In fact, maybe we should take the tape over to a police station and see what kind of equipment they have there."

Martina raised her eyebrows. "We?"

"Yeah, I'd like to know too."

"You think it might tell us something about what happened? Everyone's acting like they just want to forget about it and get on with our lives."

"I don't understand that," Cam said. "I can't figure out why they're not more curious. Nothing makes any sense. Why are we the only ones who survived? Other people were working underground. People must have been in the subways. Why haven't they survived? I thought for a while that perhaps a lethal poison was in the air, and it just didn't penetrate our room. And maybe it somehow dissolved all living organisms. But why did this poison only kill human beings? Why are animals still running around?"

She'd never before heard Cam say so much and with so much enthusiasm. She knew he was one of those guys who other kids dismissed as an intellectual nerd. He was small, slight, with wire-rimmed glasses and no-color hair—the kind of guy who passed through high school unnoticed. But he was the first person she'd talked to in a long time who was making sense. "Exactly," she said. "I think we're giving in to this too quickly." She didn't add why she believed him—that she was still convinced her sister was alive. If he was the scientific type, he'd just think she was spooky.

"Let's go now," he said.

"I don't have the tape with me. I let Travis borrow it and he hasn't given it back to me yet. In fact, I was looking for him this morning but he wasn't in his room."

"I know where he might be," Cam said.

"You do?"

"I saw him with some guys going into a diner. Maybe he's still there."

He was. From the sidewalk, they could see Travis sitting at a table with Mike, Kyle, and Andy. "What's he doing with them?" Martina wondered aloud.

"What wrong with those guys?" Cam asked.

"They're just macho jerks. They act like thugs. I thought Travis was classier."

"We can't be all that picky about who we make friends with anymore," Cam reminded her mildly. "I mean, before this happened, would you be walking down a street with me?"

She flushed. He had a point.

They went into the diner. Mike Salicki saw them first, and he coughed loudly. The others turned.

"What are you doing here?" Kyle asked in a distinctly hostile tone. Martina was taken aback. She wasn't friends with these guys, but she wasn't on their bad side, as far as she knew.

At least Travis was friendlier. "Hi, guys, what's up?" he asked easily.

Cam was looking at Andy Loomis. "What happened to you?"

Andy had a deep scratch on his face and his shirt was torn. "I was attacked by some dogs."

Martina gasped. "Are you okay?"

"Yeah, I was lucky. These guys heard me yelling and chased them away."

Travis gave Martina that obnoxious paternal look. "Now, you can see why I told you not to go out alone. Is there something you need, Martina?"

Now he was acting like the school principal. She restrained herself from pointing this out to him. "It's about that tape I gave you."

He nodded. "I listened to it, several times."

"And?"

"I didn't hear anything significant."

Martina was nonplussed. "You didn't hear someone say, 'What do you want?'"

"No, nothing like that. The voice was very clear on my cassette player. The person said, 'What do we do?'"

"What do we do?" Martina repeated.

Travis nodded. "I think it's obvious what was happening."

"You do?" Cam asked skeptically.

"Something had just happened—an explosion, a flash of light, something—and that person asked the teacher, 'What do we do?'" His expression became sad. "But of course, there was nothing anyone could do." He rose, and put an arm around Martina. "I'm sorry, Martina. I know this tape got your hopes up. But it doesn't tell us anything new."

As Martina tried to absorb this, he continued. "You know, I've asked Jake to set up a therapy group, for people who want to share their feelings about this, so they can deal with what's happened. Maybe you should talk to him."

"What do you mean, deal with what's happened?" Martina asked. "We don't know what's happened!"

There was a flicker of impatience in Travis's eyes, but he spoke kindly. "We know that everyone's gone, Martina. We're the last people on earth. And we have to come to grips with that."

Now the others were looking at Martina and Cam in annoyance, and Martina didn't think it would serve any purpose to argue with Travis. "Yeah, well, whatever. Listen, do you have the tape with you now?"

"No . . ."

"Could I come by your room and get it later? I'd like to have it back."

Now Travis actually looked embarrassed. "Oh dear, I was afraid you'd ask me that. I'm really sorry, Martina, but I guess I'm not very talented with serious stereo equipment. When I was fiddling with the controls, trying to get a clearer sound, I must have hit the wrong button. Anyway, I erased it."

She stared at him. "You erased my tape?"

"I'm sorry," he said again. "It was an accident."

What could she say?

Afterward, outside, she said to Cam, "That's weird."

"What's weird?"

"Didn't he just say he wasn't used to working with stereo equipment?"

"Yeah."

"Donna said he's very into high tech stuff."

Cam shrugged. "Most guys don't like admitting that they don't know what they're doing. Did you get a good look at the scratch on Loomis's face? Hope the dog wasn't rabid."

"Mm . . ." What Cam was saying had triggered something else in her head. Something that had been brewing ever since she'd talked to Cam in the bookstore, and he'd talked about the strangeness of their situation, the disappearance of everyone else, the survival of the animals . . . She snapped her fingers. "The animals!"

"What animals?" Cam asked.

"At the zoo! The animals at the Bronx Zoo! Oh, Cam, they haven't been fed in weeks! They're locked in those cages, it's not as if they could run around looking for food! And what about water? They could be dying of thirst!"

"I can see you feel strongly about those zoo animals," Cam remarked.

She realized how passionate she must sound. "When we were little, my sister and I used to go to the zoo all the time. We'd give the animals secret names, and we felt like we communicated with them. When I think about them now, trapped in those cages . . . no, not trapped anymore. Dead."

"Not necessarily," Cam said. "Some animals can go for a while without food. And there might have been something edible in the cages." After a moment, he added, "You want to go check it out?"

"But it's so far, all the way up in the Bronx."

"So what? You gotta be somewhere?"

They stopped back at the hotel, where they found Kesha and Donna, who also were up for a visit to the zoo. Cam had a brilliant idea—the West Side Highway, which had been closed for roadwork, was probably safe to drive on, and there wouldn't be any cars to block them. They selected a very nice BMW, and as Cam drove, Martina told the girls in the back seat about her conversation with Travis. "I really thought I heard something on that tape. Didn't you, Cam?"

Cam was tactful. "It's hard to say. There was a lot of static. I wish I could have heard it on a better machine."

"Donna, didn't you tell me Travis knows a lot about high tech stereo equipment?"

"He said he does."

Kesha let out the sniffing noise she always made when Travis's name came up. "So he either lied to you, Donna, or he lied to Martina."

"That's ridiculous," Donna said hotly. "Why would he lie about stereos? Or a dumb cassette tape?"

"Get over him, Donna," Martina sang out. But the words stayed in her head. Why would Travis lie to her? Maybe there really hadn't been anything interesting on that tape.

From the West Side Highway, they drove onto a stretch of 11th Avenue that was closed for construction. They suffered a few humongous potholes but managed to survive all the way to the Bronx. The closer they got to the zoo, the quieter everyone became. Martina thought they might be all visualizing the same awful scene that had formed in her mind—beautiful, exotic creatures, lifeless.

But they saw no dead animals at the Bronx Zoo. They saw no animals at all.

Martina stood looking into the primate house, where she and Rosa had spent many happy childhood hours naming the chimps. At first, she thought they could be hiding. But as she peered into the cages she had to realize that they just weren't there.

The others returned from various parts of the

great zoo to report the same news—the creatures had all disappeared. Just like the people.

"I can't believe you've never been to the Metropolitan Museum of Art," Jake said to Ashley as they climbed the broad steps to the museum entrance.

"I've always wanted to come," she confessed. "But I was always so busy."

Jake grinned. "Yeah, I guess putting on all that makeup takes up time."

She looked at him oddly. "I traveled a lot," she said.

"Do you miss that?" he asked.

"Not really," she admitted. "If this hadn't happened, I'd be in Milan for the fall shows, and doing fashion shoots in Rome, but all I can remember from those places are the hotels. There's other stuff I miss more."

"Like what?"

"My mother. We were very close. She was my best friend, you know. I didn't have much of a social life."

"You're kidding," he said. "You mean, Madonna wasn't your best friend?"

It seemed like a shadow came over her eyes. She didn't bother to respond to his comment, and he felt silly. He tried to make his next question more realistic. "Was there someone special in your life? Like a guy? You must have had so many guys after you."

"I never had time for that either," she replied shortly. "Wow! This room is huge!" They were in the main lobby of the museum now, and she looked around in awe.

Jake thought her reaction was interesting. This

beautiful girl had been everywhere, had lived a life none of the other kids could even imagine, but was totally awed by a place anyone could visit. "It's impossible to do the whole museum on one visit," he told her. "There's a costume exhibit, with a history of fashion."

She looked pained. "I'd rather see paintings. Just because I worked in fashion doesn't mean I'm not interested in other things."

So he took her to his favorite area, where the Impressionist paintings were displayed. She wandered through the rooms with her eyes wide. "I love those paintings that are made of little dots," she marveled. "Who painted this one?"

"That's Monet," he told her. "You've heard of Monet, haven't you?"

"No."

"He's French. You've been to France, haven't you?"

"Lots of times. But I never met him."

He laughed. "No, that wouldn't be likely. He's been dead a long time."

"Oh." She was embarrassed. "I've missed a lot of school. I must sound pretty stupid."

He was quick to reassure her. "With beauty like yours, an education in art isn't necessary. You are art."

He thought that was pretty poetic, but she wasn't impressed. In fact, she seemed a little annoyed. More than a little. "I wish you'd stop talking about the way I look," she snapped.

He was startled by the vehemence in her tone. Maybe he was coming on too strong. "You know, it's silly to leave these paintings way uptown where we can't see them. We should take some back to put up in our rooms."

"Are you saying you want to steal this art?"

"It's not like there's any other audience for them."

Her eyes lit up. "Let's do it!"

Within minutes, they had retrieved grocery carts from a nearby supermarket and brought them back into the museum. Then they went through an agonizing decision-making process as they picked out the few works they could fit into the carts.

By the time they wheeled the carts out of the museum, they were both giddy. "I feel like an international art thief," Ashley giggled.

"No one's going to miss them," Jake said.

"You really believe we're all that's left on earth?" Ashley asked.

"Looks like it to me."

"Then I guess we might as well bring this art to where the only people left on earth can see it."

"Yeah." Jake felt like there had been a shift in mood. He tried to lighten it again. "I can't believe we're going to have real art in our rooms," Jake said. "It's like a fantasy."

"Everything's like a fantasy," Ashley said. She paused at the top of the stairs and looked out over silent Fifth Avenue. "Funny, isn't it? Sometimes I think it's all a nightmare. Other times, it's a dream."

"This is dream time for me," Jake confessed.

"Because you can have all this art so close to you?"

"Not just the art. You. This could never have happened in the real world. Me with a girl like you."

The shadow crossed her eyes again, ever so briefly. Then she began to maneuver the cart carefully down the stairs. "Come on," she said. "We've got a long walk."

"It's not easy making a choice, is it?" Alex asked. He and Shalini were behind the counter in Haägen-Dazs, gazing down at the various flavors of ice cream. "This stuff isn't going to stay good forever, you know. We gotta eat a lot of it. And fast."

Shalini giggled. "I don't know which one to taste first! My father didn't allow me to have ice cream very frequently. He did not think it was healthy food."

"Boy, your old man really ran your life," Alex commented. "Telling you what you could eat, who you could marry . . . Didn't you ever want to rebel?"

"There were times I did not like his decisions," she admitted. "But he took care of me. I've never had to make any decisions on my own."

"Want me to make this decision for you?" Alex asked.

"Yes, please."

He considered the available flavors. "Try the Mint Cookies and Cream."

She did. "This is delicious!" she exclaimed happily. "Thank you for recommending it."

He grinned. "No problem." He'd never heard anyone sound so grateful before, certainly not to him. But then, Shalini wasn't like any girl he'd ever known. There was a sweetness, an innocence about her . . . Other girls at school ignored him, or eyed him warily, as if they expected him to grab their bags and run. Shalini trusted him; she needed him.

"Has your next-door neighbor been giving you

any more grief about the dog?" he asked her on the way back to the hotel. "What's his name, anyway?"

"Peppy? Oh, you mean my neighbor! He's Carlos. No, he hasn't said anything lately."

"You let me know if he bothers you," Alex declared. "I can take care of Carlos Guzman."

"Do you want to come see Peppy now?" she asked.

"Sure." He couldn't honestly say he cared all that much about the dog. But being with Shalini made him feel good.

"He starts yapping the moment he hears my footsteps," she told Alex as she opened the door to her room. "Peppy! Peppy!"

But the dog didn't come running to her, and there was no yapping. "Where is he?" she wondered. She looked under the bed and desk, then searched the closet and bathroom. "Peppy? Peppy, where are you?"

"Could he have gotten out the window?" Alex asked.

"No, it's closed."

Carlos Guzman appeared at the open door. "Hey, thanks for getting rid of that dog."

Shalini turned. "But I did not get rid of my dog! I can't find him!"

"Did you take him?" Alex demanded.

"What?"

Alex glared, and then began moving toward him. "You got in here, didn't you? And you took her dog!"

"No way, man! I'm not into dog-napping."

Aware of Shalini watching, Alex went up to Carlos and pushed him against the wall. "What did you do with her dog, you s.o.b.? Where is he?"

Carlos went red. "Take your hands off me, you ass!" He pushed back. That was all Alex needed. He slammed Carlos in the face with his fist.

Shalini screamed. That brought a couple of people out of their rooms, and suddenly Alex felt his arms being grabbed from behind.

"What's going on here?" That jerk who thought he was Master of the Universe, Darrow, appeared. Two girls came running up from the floor below.

Alex struggled to free himself. "Guzman took Shalini's dog!"

"How do you know that?" Travis wanted to know.

"He lives next door and he was the only one complaining," Alex shot back.

"I didn't take the damned dog!" Carlos yelled.

"No one took the dog." That came from Kesha Greene.

"Oh yeah?" Alex asked. "Well, he's gone! He didn't just disappear!"

"That's exactly what he did," Kesha declared. "Look outside. All the dogs are gone. And the cats, and the birds, and hopefully the roaches too."

"Are you sure about that?" Travis asked sharply.

"It must have just happened today," Kesha reported. "We went to the Bronx Zoo, and all the animals were gone. Then on the way home, we didn't see any on the streets."

Travis frowned, and his brows narrowed as if he were deep in thought. Then he spoke. "I think we'd better have a meeting tonight. Be down in the lobby. Eight o' clock."

Alex hated the way practically everyone was

looking at Travis, as if he was the acknowledged leader. Travis seemed perfectly comfortable with this. He looked like a guy in charge.

Well, he wasn't in charge of Alex, no way.

martina had already knocked on Jake's door before she realized there was a girl in there with him. Fortunately, both Jake and Ashley were fully clothed, and she'd only interrupted them in the process of hanging pictures on the wall.

"Hi," Jake said. "What's up?"

"I just wanted to make sure you knew about the meeting."

"What meeting?"

"Travis is asking the whole community to meet in the lobby at eight. To talk about what happened today."

Jake looked at her blankly. "What happened today?"

"Haven't you been outside? All the animals have disappeared!"

"Oh, yeah? I guess I didn't notice." He glanced over his shoulder at Ashley, who was positioning a painting on the wall.

"How would this look here?" she called out.

Martina peered past Jake. "Wow, that's a nice picture. It looks like a Van Gogh."

"It is a Van Gogh," Jake said. "And it's not a reproduction." He looked at his watch. "Eight o'clock, huh?" He lowered his voice. "I don't know, I might pass on it. Could you take some notes and write up an article? I could put it into the newspaper tomorrow."

"Yeah, okay." Martina left the happy couple and started downstairs. She thought she probably wouldn't see much of Jake now that he was involved with Ashley. He'd probably give up the newspaper, too, if it took him away from her. People got so single-minded when they were in love—when they thought they were in love. She thought about her sister when she had been mixed up with David. The way Donna moped over Travis. And the girls who were missing their boyfriends, who couldn't talk about anything else, who could still cry every time they heard a particular song. Would they all pair up eventually, like Jake and Ashley? And what would happen to her? She wasn't interested in any of the guys here, and certainly none of them had shown any interest in her. She'd never cared before, always assuming she'd meet Mister Right sometime, maybe in college, maybe after. It didn't look like that was a possibility anymore.

The cloud of depression she'd been dodging for weeks now settled easily on her head as she arrived in the lobby. She took a notebook and a pen out of her purse and jotted down the date.

"What are you doing?" Donna asked, sittng down next to her.

"Taking notes for the *New World*," Martina told her. "Jake's not coming. He's with Ashley Silver."

"Ooh, more gossip," Donna said. "Maybe I could write a gossip column for the newspaper."

"What other gossip have you heard?"

"Maura Kelly and David Chu. He's got a room

on my hall and she's always in there."

Martina doodled with her pen. "I just hope for her sake that she's not taking whatever he says to her too seriously."

"David's not so bad," Donna said. "He's just a playboy. And I don't think Maura takes anything too seriously."

Watching Maura bounce into the lobby a few minutes later, she had to wonder about that. She certainly seemed carefree. Handsome David Chu sauntered in a moment later and sat beside her. But he was watching the door, and smiling every time a girl came in. Maura didn't seem to care.

Maybe Donna was right, and Maura wouldn't be devastated the way Rosa had been when David dumped her and moved on to someone else, but she still thought Donna was wrong when she said David wasn't so bad. She remembered how Rosa had felt. David Chu was dangerous, and not to be trusted.

She was distracted from her thoughts by the sound of Travis calling the meeting to order. He stood by the fireplace, the focal point of the large room. But he wasn't standing there alone. Mike Salicki stood on one side of him, and Kyle Bailey was on his other side.

"You guys might have heard about some events that have occurred in the past couple of days," Travis told the group. Most of what he had to say Martina already knew, about the dog attack on Andy, and the animals disappearing. But there was other news.

"Jimmy DuPont was jogging alone around Washington Square Park," Travis told them. "He tripped and hurt his ankle, bad. He couldn't even walk. It was pure luck that a couple of guys were walking through the park and saw him. He's going to be okay, but if those guys hadn't found him, he could be lying there still. He could be dead."

He paused to let those words sink in, and then continued. "There was another troubling incident. Heather, would you tell the community about it?"

A girl rose. "I was at the health club, the one across the street. When I was near the swimming pool, I heard some splashing so I looked in to see who was there. Courtney had just jumped off the diving board, and she was just floating on the surface. She must have hit her head."

There was a gasp in the crowd. "Is she okay?" someone asked.

"She almost drowned," Heather said importantly. "I jumped in and got her out just in time."

"This is a warning for all of us," Travis said. "Like I said when we first tried to get organized, we have to look out for each other. But maybe we need to make that more regulated. I asked Mike here to start up a buddy system. Mike, tell everyone about it."

The brawny, slack-jawed boy with the buzz cut stepped forward. He folded his arms across his chest, which Martina thought gave him an ominous look. "I'm asking some guys to be offical buddies, to go places with people so they don't have to go anywhere alone."

"It's for the safety and protection of the community," Travis interjected. "Anything can happen."

A belligerent voice spoke out. "Maybe some of us can protect ourselves. And our friends." Martina, busily taking notes, turned to see who had spoken. It was Alex Popov, and he definitely looked hostile.

Travis shook his head solemnly. "I hear you. No one wants to admit to being vulnerable. But I don't care how big and strong and independent any of us are. There are dangers out there. Dangers we know about, and . . . maybe some dangers we don't know about. Like, what made those animals disappear today?"

"Maybe the dog that attacked Andy got an infection and spread it around," someone yelled, and there was a wave of laughs.

Travis smiled patiently. "Very funny. Seriously, folks, some of you have asked me to help organize the community and that's what I'm trying to do. I'm thinking that we could assign buddies to be on duty at the health club, and other places." There was a smattering of applause.

"There have also been some reports of loud parties and other disturbances in this building," Travis went on. "I'm going to ask the Buddies to keep an eye out for these disturbances, and break up groups that are disturbing other people. You can always take your parties somewhere else. People want peace and quiet here." He got another round of applause, louder and more enthusiastic.

Martina watched Travis thoughtfully. He was definitely taking his responsibilities seriously.

"He's taking himself too seriously," Kesha stated after the meeting broke up. "He sounds like he thinks he's completely in charge."

That's how he had sounded to Martina, too. "He's just one person, how much control can he have?"

"But now he's got goons like Mike and Kyle on his side," Kesha pointed out. "I don't like that."

Actually, Martina wasn't too crazy about having creeps like Mike and Kyle acting as a protection force for the group. But she didn't want to fuel Kesha's paranoia. "We'll see," was all she said. And she went back to her room to write up the newspaper article.

Jake sat at his desk and wrote.

She just left, because she said she was tired. I can't blame her, after that eighty-block walk today. She's wonderful, I can't take my eyes off her. Never in a million years had I thought that a girl like that would ever look twice at me. I know that if circumstances were different, if we were back in the old world at Madison High, we wouldn't be starting up this relationship. But I don't care. I can live like this with a girl like Ashley.

He put down his pen, closed his eyes and let the images appear as if on a movie screen in his head. He and Ashley, in a wedding ceremony, roaming the world together on a honeymoon, having beautiful children to repopulate the earth.

A scratching sound interrupted his fantasies. Some papers had been slipped under his door. He got up and retrieved them

It was Martina's article for the *New World*, about the meeting. He'd read it tomorrow. He'd rather daydream tonight.

But he wasn't going to have that luxury. Only seconds later, there was a knock on his door.

It was Kesha. "We have to talk," she said.

"About what?"

Kesha didn't wait for an invitation. She walked in and sat down on Jake's bed. "About Travis."

Jake groaned. This was getting tiresome. "Oh, Kesha, enough about Travis. Give it up."

"No, you have to hear this. He's setting up a private police force."

Jake forced himself to listen. "Kesha, come on, you're exaggerating—"

"And did you hear how he erased Martina's tape?"

He picked up Martina's report then, and quickly scanned it. "There's nothing about a tape here."

"She found it at school and she heard something that made her suspicious."

"What?"

"I don't know, she didn't tell me. But whatever it was, don't you think it's interesting that Travis didn't hear it? And now the tape is erased, so nobody can hear it."

"That doesn't mean he did it on purpose," Jake said.

Kesha ignored that. "And now there's this police squad."

Jake glanced at the report. "Buddy system."

"Whatever. It means the same thing. Mike Salicki is in charge. And after the meeting, I saw him talking to Ryan and Scott."

"So what?"

"Don't you see what that means? Those are the biggest guys in the group. The most athletic. Travis is getting all the physical power on his side."

In another room, someone had turned up a stereo system. Jake had to raise his voice. "I think you're jumping to conclusions," he stated.

"Come on, Jake, you know what he's like. Travis is a politician. Do you actually trust him?"

Jake let out a weary sigh. "So what are you planning to do?"

"I want you to do something," Kesha said. "I want you to talk to Travis, find out what his motives are."

Jake blinked. "Me? Why me?"

"Well, I can't. If I criticize Travis, he'll think it's because I'm still holding a grudge over losing that dumb election to him."

"Then ask someone else."

The music from across the hall was getting louder. "Who?" Kesha practically screamed. "Donna can't do it, she's still got a crush on him. Travis wouldn't pay any attention to someone like Cam, I'm sure he thinks Cam's a wuss. But I think he'd listen to you. He respects you."

Jake smiled, but he shook his head. "I'm not your guy, Kesha. I'm not the political type."

"You don't have to be political," Kesha said. "You just have to care. Don't you care what happens to us?"

He was spared having to answer. From out in the hall, there was an unusually loud banging sound. They both went to the door and looked out.

Kyle Bailey was pounding on Andy Loomis's door. As they watched, Andy opened it.

"Turn down that stereo," Kyle ordered him

"Yeah, yeah, okay," Andy muttered, and slammed the door. A second later, the volume was lower.

"Thanks," Jake called to him.

"No problem," Kyle said. It was then that Jake noticed a strip of red cloth wrapped around Kyle's upper right arm.

"What's that?"

"Mike Salicki's giving them out, to all the Buddies. So people will know who we are."

"Like a police badge?" Kesha asked innocently.

"Yeah, I guess so." He sauntered away.

Kesha looked at Jake meaningfully. But Jake wouldn't take the bait.

"Look, at least I'll be able to sleep," Jake said. " 'Night, Kesha." And he shut the door.

nine

In the lobby, Martina laid out the twenty-five copies of the *New World*. She checked over her own article, and was pleased to see that Jake hadn't changed anything. Of course, he might not even have read it. The good of the community wasn't his highest priority right now.

The rest of the newspaper was made up of announcements. Someone was trying to organize a theater group. A soccer team was forming. Some idiot was asking for nominations for prom queen and king.

"It's like they're trying to reinvent high school."

She turned to see Cam reading over her shoulder. "You can have your own copy," she said.

"No thanks," he replied. "I never much liked the real high school. I'm not interested in any facsimile version."

She had to smile.

"What about you?" he asked. "How do you feel about the new society Travis is creating?"

"I'd rather have the old one back." She looked at him. He wasn't laughing.

"I had an idea," he said. "I was thinking about your tape."

"Do you think we should go back to school and see if we can find another one?" she asked him. "Maybe there was another student who didn't hear well."

"I was thinking of security cameras. Lots of stores have them, you know. To catch shoplifters. Banks have them, too. And there are tapes in the cameras that run all the time. Which means—"

Martina finished for him. "Whatever happened— it could be on a video tape!"

"Exactly," Cam said.

She couldn't believe this hadn't occurred to her earlier. "Let's go."

They went to the first grocery store they came to. "Oh, that smell," Martina gasped.

"Rotting food," Cam noted.

She felt positively ill. "Can't we go to a bank instead?"

"Hang on a sec." Cam had spotted a camera. Taking a pole that was used to get products off high shelves, he began attacking the camera until it broke away from the wall and clattered to the ground.

"Let's go," Martina hissed, clapping a hand to her mouth before she could vomit. Back out on the street, she took in a deep breath of relatively clean-smelling air while Cam pried the tape out of the camera.

"You want to look for more?" he asked.

Martina was still feeling nauseated. "Let's go back and watch this one first."

Back in the hotel, Andy Loomis was standing just inside the main door. "How's the scratch on your face?" Martina asked him.

"It's better," Andy said. "Where have you two been?"

"Just out," Cam said quickly.

"Out where?"

His tone was oddly insistent, and Martina was puzzled. "Why do you want to know?"

"It's the new policy," Andy said. "Everyone's supposed to sign in and out and say where they're going." He showed them a neatly designed sheet of paper with spaces for names, destinations, and times in and out.

"When did this happen?" Martina asked in bewilderment.

"About ten minutes ago," Andy told her. "It's Travis's idea. That way, he can know where everyone is."

Martina's brow furrowed. "Why does Travis need to know where everyone is?"

"Safety, protection," Andy said vaguely. "He made me one of the Buddies, see?" He indicated the red band on his arm. "They were hassling me about playing my stereo too loud. I figured, if you can't beat 'em, join 'em."

Martina looked at the paper again. "What do I have to do?"

"Just write down where you went, what time you went and what time you got back."

"We didn't sign out," Cam said. "I don't see why we should have to sign in."

" 'Cause it's the rule," Andy said impatiently. He noticed the video in Cam's hand. "Where were you, the video store?"

"That's right," Cam said. He scrawled that down on the paper. "Come on, Martina."

"Why did you lie about the tape?" Martina asked him in the elevator.

"I'm not sure," Cam said. "I don't like being interrogated, I guess."

Martina examined the tape. "Should we take this to my room? I have a VCR."

"So do I," Cam said. "And a giant-screen TV."

"There was a giant-screen TV in your room?"

"No, I went out and got one from a store."

"But there's nothing on TV," Martina pointed out.

"I watch videos. Lots of videos. I've seen the *Star Wars* trilogy fifty times. Of course, it's best to see it on a real movie screen."

Cam had decorated his hotel room. She walked around to look at his pictures and posters. A huge *X-Files* poster proclaimed *I want to believe*. A series of four posters displayed the casts of *Star Trek*, *Star Trek: The Next Generation*, *Star Trek: Deep Space Nine*, and *Star Trek: Voyager*. There was a framed copy of the front page of a newspaper from the 1950s. The headline read ALIEN LANDING IN ROSWELL, NEW MEXICO? In what appeared to be a place of honor on the bookcase was a framed, autographed photo of Mr. Spock.

It made Martina a little uneasy. So Cam was into science fiction and the paranormal. No wonder he was so interested in finding out what had happened. When he ejected the tape that was currently in the VCR, she caught a glimpse of the title: *Alien Autopsy: Fact or Fiction?* Then he put in the tape they'd taken from the grocery, punched REWIND, and turned on the TV. They were both silent as they waited for the tape to rewind. Then Cam hit PLAY.

There was some fuzz, and a picture came up on the screen, a poor quality black and white image of empty grocery store aisles. Then a man could be seen at the door. He appeared to be unlocking it. He left camera range for a minute, and then reappeared behind the checkout counter. He opened what looked like a magazine.

For what had to be at least a couple of minutes, Martina and Cam watched him read his magazine. "Should I fast forward it?" Cam wondered.

"Wait," Martina said. "Look. Something's happening."

The door was opening, and a woman holding a child's hand came in. Martina watched as she picked up a shopping basket, and began walking down an aisle. She took things off the shelves—a box of something, a can of something else, a bag of what might have been potatoes or onions. She placed each item in the basket. At one point, the child pointed to the candy display. The woman shook her head. The child's mouth opened wide for a silent scream.

"Turn up the volume," Martina said.

"I don't think there's any sound on security tapes," Cam replied. He played around with the remote, but the film remained silent.

The woman went to the checkout counter with her basket. She gave money to the man standing there, and he put her purchases in a bag. The woman and the child left the store. The man went back to his magazine.

"Well, that wasn't very revealing," Martina commented. "How long does this tape last anyway?"

"I'm not sure," Cam replied. "Maybe eight hours?" He moved closer to the screen and studied it. "You see those numbers in the upper right-hand corner of the screen?"

"Yeah, what are they?"

"I think it's some kind of counter. It shows how

much time is passing. What time do these stores usually open?"

Martina edged closer to the screen. "About eight o'clock, I think."

"What time did fifth period start at school?"

"Twelve forty-five."

Cam hit the FAST FORWARD button. Like an old-time movie, people raced in and out of the store, and ran up and down the aisles. Items flew off the shelves. When the counter reached four hours and forty-five minutes, Cam punched PLAY and the tape went back into normal motion.

For a while, the action went on as it had before. People came in, made purchases, and left. The man at the checkout counter went through several magazines.

Then a customer, who appeared to be examining the label of a can, looked up suddenly, in a direction beyond camera range. The can dropped from his hand.

A woman with her back to the camera must have heard the sound of the can hitting the floor. She whirled around and faced in that same direction. She clasped a hand to her mouth, as if to muffle a cry. Then every person Martina could see on the screen was looking in that direction. As distorted and fuzzy as the picture was, there was no mistaking the similarity of their expressions: Horror. Terror. And then the screen went dark.

They waited a few seconds, but nothing more appeared. Eerily, the tape showed the same scene as in its first few moments, before the store opened.

"Play it again," Martina whispered, but Cam had already anticipated her request and had begun rewinding.

They watched it again, and then again. The third time, Cam stopped the tape just as the man was dropping the can. The frame froze, with the can in midair. "Do you see that?"

"What?"

"That darkness, in the lower left-hand corner. There." He touched the screen. "It wasn't there a few seconds ago."

"Are you sure?"

Cam let the tape rewind for a second. Then he moved it forward, frame by frame. "See?"

Martina looked closely. The area in the lower left-hand corner did seem to darken from one frame to the next. "It could be a scratch on the tape," she said doubtfully. "Or maybe something was spilled on it."

"No, I think it's part of the picture," Cam said.

"Can you do something with the contrast so we can see it more clearly?" Martina asked.

Cam fiddled with the dials. Then he shook his head. "It's a fancy screen, but it's just an ordinary basic television."

Once again, he went through that section of the video frame by frame. "The dark area, it gets larger," he noted. "As if it's coming closer to the people."

"But that's not what the people are looking at," Martina pointed out. "See, look where their eyes are focused. They're looking just right of the shadow."

"That's it!" Cam exclaimed. "It's a shadow! A shadow of whatever they're looking at!"

Martina could barely breathe. "Yes . . . yes, I think you're right."

*   *   *

"I've never been in Brooklyn before," Ashley told Jake as they walked up Eastern Parkway. "I'm having all kinds of firsts with you."

Jake had never felt so amazingly happy. He felt like he was having firsts too. He'd probably walked across the Brooklyn Bridge a hundred times in his life, but he'd never crossed it with Ashley Silver before. Under other circumstances, he probably would have found the walk down Flatbush Avenue depressing, but not with Ashley. It was as if her beauty made everything look better. Sometimes, he regretted the fact that there was no one around to see him with her. On the other hand, it was awfully nice having her all to himself.

And, of course, there was the biggest first—his first love.

"I don't know what the Botanic Garden will look like, since no one's been taking care of it," he cautioned as he led her toward the entrance. But he needn't have worried. Whatever had happened in this world, it hadn't affected the fall foliage or the growth of autumn flowers.

"Oh, how lovely!" Ashley gasped as they moved through the bucolic gardens, with their lawns and flowering shrubs. "Isn't this the most gorgeous sight in the universe?"

"No," Jake said. "You are."

The compliment didn't please her. "Jake, would you please stop talking about how I look?"

He was startled. "Why?"

"Because I'm sick of it! When I was modeling, all anyone ever talked about was how I looked. I'm a person, Jake! Can't you think of me as something other than a face and a body?"

He was ashamed. He'd always considered himself a modern man, someone who didn't put women in categories like some of the macho jerks at school. "I'm sorry," he said humbly.

"I forgive you." They spent the next hour gloriously running through the gardens, walking on grass they weren't supposed to walk on, stepping over a chain fence so they could get a closer look at some late autumn roses. Ashley was enraptured by the Japanese garden, where they ate a picnic of crackers and cheese and wine. After lunch, they fell asleep under a weeping willow tree. Jake awoke to find Ashley in his arms. When she opened her eyes, she didn't pull away.

After that, it seemed natural to hold hands while walking back, and to kiss in the center of the Brooklyn Bridge while the last rays of the sun glowed around them. The euphoria stayed with them all the way back into Manhattan.

Then they returned to the hotel, where the golden haze evaporated the very moment they walked into the lobby.

Scott Spivey, someone Jake had never spoken to in his entire life, stood there with his hand up. "Halt!"

Both Ashley and Jake were so startled by the unexpected command that they actually froze. "Names?"

Jake looked at him in amusement. Maybe they weren't friends, but they'd been living in the same building for almost four weeks. "You know our names."

"Names?" He was blocking their way.

What kind of game was this? Obviously, if they didn't play along they weren't going to get any farther into the building. "Jake Robbins and Ashley Silver."

Scott made an elaborate show of looking over a

paper attached to a clipboard. "You're not on the list."

"The list for what?" Ashley asked. "What is this, backstage at a Michael Jackson concert?"

"You're supposed to sign out when you leave the building and sign in when you return."

"You're not serious," Jake said.

"It's the law," Scott informed him.

"Since when?" Jake wanted to know. "And who's making these laws?"

Scott ignored the questions. "I'll let you off this time. Just tell me what time you left, and where you were."

Now Jake was annoyed. "That's none of your damn business."

"You don't think so?" Scott indicated his red armband. "I'm a Buddy, man."

"Well, you're not my buddy," Jake growled. Still holding Ashley's hand, he started past Scott. Suddenly, he was slammed back to the wall. Ashley practically fell.

"Hey, you stupid moron, what the hell do you think you're doing!" Jake screamed. At his voice, Mike Salicki appeared from a door behind the hotel registration desk.

"What's going on?"

"This jerk won't follow rules!" Scott declared hotly.

Mike moved very close to Jake, practically into his face. "What's your problem, Robbins? You didn't hear about the new rules? You must have left early this morning."

"We did," Jake said through clenched teeth.

"Where did you go?"

Ashley spoke. "Brooklyn Botanic Gardens."

Mike frowned. "You left Manhattan?"

"What's the matter, is that against the rules?" Jake retorted.

Mike took the clipboard from Scott and jotted something down. "Not yet."

"Can we go now?" Ashley asked.

"Yeah," Mike said. "But be a little more cooperative next time."

Jake could feel Ashley's hand gripping his tightly as they waited for the elevator. They didn't speak until they were inside and the doors had closed.

Ashley was in a state of shock. "What was that all about?"

"That was creepy," Jake said. "That was very, very creepy."

"I guess it's supposed to be for our own good," Ashley murmured, but she didn't sound too convinced of her own words.

"Do you know Kesha Greene?" he asked suddenly.

"Not really. Why?"

"I think I need to speak to her."

When Kesha opened her door, Jake spoke abruptly. "I owe you an apology."

"For what?" Kesha said.

"For saying you were being paranoid about Travis. Ashley and I just got the treatment from one of those idiot Buddies. It made me sick."

"Come on in," Kesha said. Once inside the room, he saw that Kesha wasn't alone. Cam, Martina, and Donna were sitting on the floor, eating taco chips and salsa dip. "Join us," she said.

Jake looked at Ashley. Taco chips didn't seem like her style. She was probably accustomed to caviar and champagne. But she sat down on the rug with the others and dug in.

Jake couldn't eat; he was still fuming. "You know what I was thinking about when that Salicki ass was interrogating us? Did you ever see the movie *Schindler's List*?"

"Oh, you're getting carried away," Donna remonstrated. "Those guys, they're acting like pompous asses, but they're not exactly Nazis. I mean, come on, these are guys we go to school with!"

"Who do you think the Nazis were?" Kesha asked her. "They were just guys other people went to school with, too."

"Look," Jake said. "I'm not calling them Nazis, and I'm not saying that Travis is turning into Hitler. But this is how dictatorships get started. Someone with lots of charisma, like Travis, comes forward in a time of trouble and uncertainty. He preys on people's fears, he appeals to them. They put their faith in him. And then he's got real power."

Kesha's head was bobbing up and down in agreement. But Donna still looked troubled. "When I used to go with Travis, it wasn't the best relationship in the world. But he was always nice."

Cam spoke to her kindly. "Travis is a very likable guy. That's what makes him dangerous."

"He's presenting himself as a father figure," Martina said. "Someone who can protect us and take care of us. But that's not the kind of leader we need right now."

"What kind of leader do you think we need?" Ashley asked her.

Kesha answered that. "Someone with curiosity. Someone who isn't afraid to find out what really happened."

"Someone like you?" Donna asked with a teasing smile.

But Kesha shook her head. "No, I lost one election to Travis already. Nobody's going to listen to me." She was looking directly at Jake.

"Whoa, stop right there," Jake said. "Don't look at me."

"You could be an alternative to Travis," Kesha said.

"I'm not a leader," Jake said. "Besides, what could I offer people that Travis isn't offering?"

Kesha looked at Martina, Cam, and Donna. It was clear to Jake that they'd been discussing this before he arrived.

Martina spoke. "Travis is basically telling us that we have to accept our situation and cope with it. Right?"

"I guess so," Jake said.

"Maybe your position could be that we need to go beyond that, that we shouldn't give up so easily. Instead of simply accepting the situation, we should maybe try to resolve it. And learn the truth."

Jake wasn't quite sure he was catching on to her meaning. "Do you know something I don't know?"

"Show the tape," Kesha said to Cam.

"It would be better on my giant screen," Cam said, "but this should give you something to think about."

As he adjusted the tape, Martina explained how they'd recovered the security tape. Then Cam played it for them. He showed them the last thirty seconds frame by frame, pointing out the shadow, the expressions on people's faces, and the direction of their eyes.

"They're not looking outside," Ashley remarked.

"No," Cam said. "It looks like something . . . or someone . . . appeared in that store."

"But not just there," Martina remarked.

Cam agreed. "Maybe something appeared in all stores, in homes, on streets, all over the world. In any case, it doesn't look like a bomb."

"What are you going to do with that tape?" Jake asked.

"We're not sure yet," Cam said. "After the way Travis erased Martina's cassette, I'm not turning it over to him."

"That was an accident," Donna murmured, but no one paid any attention.

"If I were you," Jake said, "I'd want to take the tape to a photo lab, enlarge the frames. Maybe there's a way to get a sharper focus on the shape and form of the shadow."

Ashley spoke up. "We could go out and collect more surveillance tapes from stores. Then we might be able to see the shadows from other angles." After a moment, she added, "Or maybe see what's making the shadow."

Kesha was looking at her with approval. "Funny, I never would have thought you'd be on our side."

"Travis, you're editing the newspaper," Martina said. "Maybe you could write an editorial. We could find out if other people are happy about Travis's new rules."

"Wait a minute," Jake said hastily. "Let's not get carried away. Take one step at a time. Let's just see what we can learn from this video, and any other ones we can find. We don't need to talk about who's going to challenge Travis or what side anyone's on. It's not like we're at war."

Kesha eyed him steadily. "Not yet."

cam wanted to take the video tape to a photo lab first thing in the morning. But when Martina met him in the hotel lobby, he was studying an announcement. "New rules," he told Martina.

"What kind of new rules?"

"It's not enough to sign in and out anymore. You have to be accompanied by a Buddy when you leave the hotel."

"You're not serious!" She read the announcement for herself. "Geez, you are serious. This can't be for real."

"Here comes Travis now, why don't you ask him about it?"

Travis wasn't alone. Two red-armbanded guys accompanied him. "Travis," Martina called out, starting toward him. Immediately, the two guys stepped in front of Travis, effectively blocking Martina from getting any closer to him.

Martina raised her hands in mock surrender. "Hey, I'm not dangerous! You can frisk me, I'm not even armed!"

Travis laughed. "I'm sorry, Martina. I've been getting some strange notes lately, and Mike's insisting I take Buddies with me everywhere."

"What kind of notes?"

Travis waved a hand dismissively. "Crank stuff. Someone's not happy about the new rules."

One of the bodyguards spoke. "We think it's that Commie, Popov. He's always complaining."

Travis looked at him reprovingly. "Scott, don't make accusations when you don't have any proof."

"We'll get proof," Scott said.

"Actually, I was wondering about this new rule," Martina said, indicating the announcement. "Is this really necessary?"

"I think so, for the time being," Travis told her. "It's for our own protection."

"Travis, we're not children," Martina protested. "We can—"

But Travis wasn't interested in her comments. With guards on either side, he moved on.

"So how are we going to get that video to the photo lab?" Cam asked her.

"I have to think," Martina said. She was momentarily distracted by the appearance of Maura.

"Look!" Maura chirped. She was wearing a red armband. "I'm the first girl Buddy!"

"Congratulations," Martina muttered.

"I wish we had uniforms, that would be so cool! I feel so totally not pulled together. Do you know how long it's been since I had a real manicure? And look at my hair! It's a disaster!"

Martina wanted to get away to talk privately with Cam. "Looks fine, Maura. I have to run—"

"Oh puh-leeze!" Maura screeched. "I've got roots a mile long!"

The girl was too pathetic. "Don't worry about it," Martina said. "I'm sure David doesn't care."

Maura tossed her multicolored hair. "David is history. You know, it's really a shame. I co to the fanciest, most expensive salon in New York now. Only there's nobody who knows how to do anything with hair."

"I do," Martina said suddenly.

"What?"

"My mother was a hairdresser. I can cut, and color, and give perms . . ."

Maura's mouth fell open. "Really? Oh, Martina, could you do something with my hair?"

Martina could feel the excitement rising within her. "Sure. Meet me at two o'clock, we'll go to a salon. Oh—wait. I guess we have to take a Buddy with us."

"No we don't, I am a Buddy, remember?"

"Why did you offer to do that?" Cam asked Martina when they were alone on the elevator.

"Don't you see? We'll take the tape with us, and I'll take Maura to a salon on Nineteenth Street. There are photo labs around there. After I put some stuff on Maura's hair, I'll tell her the salon is out of something I need and I have to go get it from another salon. She won't want to come with me because her hair will be covered with gook and she'll look terrible. You'll meet me at the lab."

"How am I going to get out of this place without a Buddy?" Cam wanted to know.

She looked at him critically. "You know, you could use a haircut too."

She thought it was a brilliant plan. At lunch, she told Kesha, Donna, Jake, and Ashley about it. Jake wasn't as enthusiastic. "Maura's not going to just sit there alone while you and Cam run off."

"I'll stay with her," Ashley volunteered. "She's always asking me these dumb questions about my glamorous life as a model. She'll be more than happy to stay if I'm there."

"But what's your excuse for being there?" Martina asked.

Ashley shrugged. "I don't care, you can give me a perm or something."

Jake looked at her in dismay. "Are you sure you want to get involved?"

"Of course I'm sure," Ashley said. "If Martina can get involved, why can't I?"

"Because I'm not in love with Martina," Jake blurted out. Then his face went red as everyone else at the table had a good laugh.

Alex knew it couldn't be Shalini knocking on his door. She couldn't pound that hard. "Who is it?" he called out.

"Open the door or we'll break it down!"

Alex went to the door and opened it. Two guys with red armbands stood there.

"What do you want?" Alex asked.

"We're searching your room," one of them declared. They pushed past him and walked in.

"Hey!" Alex cried out in rage. "You can't do this!"

They ignored him. One guy went into his closet, while the other began opening desk drawers. Both of them were pulling things out and throwing them on the floor. Aghast, but aware that he couldn't take on the two of them, Alex watched in horror.

"What the hell do you think you're doing?"

"Let me see your wallet," one of the guys demanded.

"What for?"

"You got a driver's license?"

"Yeah, why?"

"I want to see your signature."

Seething, about to explode, Alex reached in his

pocket and took out his wallet. The guy grabbed it out of his hand, opened it, and took out the driver's license. He handed it to the other guy. "What do you think?"

He compared it to some writing on a paper. Finally, he said, "Nah."

"What's going on?" Alex demanded to know.

But it was as if he wasn't there. The guy tossed his wallet on the floor, and they walked out.

Once they left, Alex remained standing, clenching his fists, feeling the blood and the fury rise to his face. Once he was able to feel somewhat in control of his body, he went to Shalini's room.

When she opened the door, he spoke abruptly. "I'm getting out of here. I don't know where I'm going, but I'm getting out. You want to come with me?"

Maura was delighted to learn that Ashley would be going to the salon with them. "I've been dying to talk to you," she gushed. "How did you get discovered? Do you absolutely have to be tall to be a model? How much do you weigh?"

The beauty salon on 19th Street was twenty blocks away. Maura chattered nonstop throughout the half hour walk.

"I saw a photo of you in the *National Enquirer* with that guy from *Melrose Place*, the one who plays Billy. What's he really like?"

Ashley was being extraordinarily patient. "I don't remember, I only met him once, at a club in Beverly Hills. Some photographer took a picture of us. The next thing I knew, the magazines had us practically married!"

She spoke as if she was sharing some remarkable secret, and Maura giggled appreciatively.

"Oh wow, you have the most incredible life. Have you ever met Brad Pitt? Is he as gorgeous in person as in the movies?"

She went on and on in this vein. Ashley handled the barrage of stupid questions very nicely, and Martina was impressed. Cam didn't say much. He kept tugging nervously on his shaggy hair.

They turned onto 19th Street now, and were approaching the salon, Hair Today. Martina could see two photo labs just beyond it.

"Why did you pick this salon?" Maura wanted to know.

"My mother worked here for a while," Martina lied. "It's got good equipment, and I know where everything is."

She directed Ashley and Maura to side by side stations. From where they were sitting, Maura wouldn't be able to see Martina searching the salon for the items she needed. It didn't matter— Maura wasn't watching her. She was still caught up in asking Ashley about the celebrities she'd met.

Ashley regaled Maura with information about a certain supermodel who was noted for throwing tantrums, while Martina put the lightener on Maura's hair. When she finished, she applied the permanent solution to Ashley's hair and wound it on rollers.

"Now I'll cut Cam's hair," she said. She went back to the supply cabinet and counted to ten. Then she yelled, "Oh, no!"

"What's the matter?" Ashley called out.

"I can't find the right shade of toner for Maura's hair!"

Maura shrieked. "I thought you said this place would have everything!"

"Well, they're out of toner number 53. Look, don't panic, I'm sure there are other salons around here. I'll just run out and look around."

"You can't go wandering around by yourself!" Maura protested.

"Cam, would you come with me?" Martina asked sweetly. To Maura she said, "I know he's not an official Buddy, but at least he's a guy."

That rationale satisfied Maura.

"Gee, couldn't you give me my haircut first?" Cam asked. "What if we run into someone?"

"Oh, shut up," Martina muttered. They took off.

In the first photo lab they came to, Cam took the video from Martina and carefully removed the actual tape from the plastic container. He placed the tape under something that resembled a microscope. Slowly, he began to adjust the dials and move the tape.

"Can you see anything?" Martina asked him.

"Not yet."

Martina kept her eyes on the clock. After a moment, she asked, "See anything now?"

"Martina, I'll tell you when I see something."

"Well, I can't leave that junk on their hair forever," Martina commented. She forced herself to keep quiet as Cam adjusted dials. Then he said, "Look at this."

He stepped aside and let Martina peer through the lens. "What am I supposed to be looking at?"

"Keep your eye on the shadow."

The dark blur was becoming more distinct. Now it had a shape—a shape that suggested a head, arms, legs . . . "It's a person," she said in wonderment.

"You think so? You ever seen a human being make a shadow like that? Now, watch."

He touched the dials and everything went dark.

"What did you just do?"

"I moved to the next frame. Look at it for a while."

"It's blank. There's nothing to look at."

"Keep looking."

As her eyes adjusted, she realized that parts of the frame were darker than other parts. Something was there, a picture, but it was too dark for her to make it out. "Can you lighten it?"

"Maybe." Cam took the piece of film and dipped it into a solution. Martina gnawed on a fingernail as Cam watched the second hand on the clock. Then he removed the tape from the liquid.

"I should let this air-dry," he muttered. "But that could take a while."

"I can't stay away from the salon much longer," Martina told him. "Maura's going to get suspicious."

Cam located something that looked like a miniature fan. He aimed it at the piece of tape for a few minutes and let air blow on it. Then he put it under the microscope thing again.

He lifted his head. "Look."

Martina peered through the microscope. She saw the same image she'd seen before—the customers with shock on their faces looking at the shadow.

"Now, watch carefully," Cam said. He moved to the next frame. It was the same picture, but the customers looked duller. He touched the dial again, and now they looked even dimmer. Then they looked almost transparent.

"Does this remind you of something?" he asked. She wasn't sure.

He touched the dial again. Now she could literally see through the customers' bodies. Then they were gone.

"What does it mean?" she asked.

"You ever watch *Star Trek*?"

"Of course, why?"

"Do you remember how characters were beamed from one place to another, through molecular transfiguration? Remember how they looked when they were being beamed? Doesn't this look like that?"

"Cam, that's television, it's fantasy."

"It's science fiction," Cam corrected her. "It's fantasy based on science. What that show demonstrated wasn't fairy tale magic, it was an extrapolation of known scientific phenomena."

"Huh?"

"That TV show predicted future technological achievements based on what we know to be scientifically possible."

She thought she understood what he was saying, but she was still confused. "Cam, what's going on in this video?"

"Those people we see . . . they don't look like they're dying, Martina. They look like they're going somewhere."

when martina returned to the salon, Maura was not happy. "What took you so long? My scalp is burning."

At the supply cabinet, Martina grabbed the toner number 53 which had been there all along. "Sorry," she said as she rinsed the lightener out of Maura's hair. "You wouldn't believe this, every salon was out of this toner. It must be the most popular shade in town. I had to go to six salons. There were other shades of blond, but I knew you wanted something closer to platinum than gold." She knew she was prattling inanely, and Ashley was eyeing her curiously, but all Martina wanted to do at this point was finish her job here, get back to the residence, and report what they'd seen to the others.

She applied the toner to Maura's hair. "Now, you only have to wait twenty minutes for this to work."

She moved on to Ashley. "Your hair should be nice and wavy by now," she said hopefully. She began unwinding a curler. When the plastic cylinder was out of Ashley's hair and in Martina's hand, she knew right away that something was wrong. A lock of golden brown hair clung to the curler.

Ashley could see Martina's expression in the mirror. "What's the matter?"

"I think I might have left the solution in too long," Martina said weakly. She began to unroll another curler. Another lock of hair accompanied it.

Maura turned to look. She shrieked. "Ashley, your hair's falling out!"

Rapidly, Martina began taking out curlers. She worked as gently as possible. But with each curler, a chunk of hair left Ashley's head.

She waited for Ashley to begin screaming. But while the pretty girl definitely looked startled as the hair came off her head, she didn't go berserk.

"I'm sorry," Martina wailed. "Truly, I'm so very sorry, Ashley!"

Ashley remained calm. She began to watch with interest as her new coiffure—her lack of coiffure—emerged. "Well," she said finally. "It will be easy to take care off."

Martina was in a state of shock and guilt. "I'm so sorry!"

"It's just hair," Ashley said. "It will grow back." She examined herself critically. "I look like that Irish singer. Let's shave off the little clumps that are left."

Martina's hands were shaking as she followed Ashley's orders. What she found really amazing was the fact that Ashley was still beautiful. Bald, but beautiful.

Martina couldn't believe she was being so cool about it. Apparently, the girl wasn't anywhere near as vain as Martina had thought a model would be. Her opinion of Ashley soared.

Fortunately, Maura's hair turned out fine. Martina doubted that she would have been as understanding as Ashley. All the way home, Maura was looking at Ashley in horror. "Maybe you'll start a new style," was all she could say, and she said it doubtfully.

Back in the residence, they ran into Donna and Kesha in the lobby. When they saw Ashley, Donna looked aghast, but Kesha was cool. "That's fantastic," she declared. "Martina, could you shave my head like that?"

Donna recovered from her shock. "Me too," she chimed in, with just a little too much enthusiasm.

Then Jake appeared. When he saw Ashley, he went white, and it took a moment before he could actually say, "What happened?"

"It's okay," Ashley assured him. "Actually, I like it. It's very comfortable."

But Jake was very upset. He walked around Ashley, shaking his head. "Well, at least it happened now, and not before."

"What do you mean?"

"It's not like you've got a career now. This would have totally destroyed it."

Ashley shrugged.

"I'm really sorry," Jake said. "I know this has to be killing you." He paused to shoot a furious look at Martina. "Honestly, Ashley, I didn't think something like this could happen." He clutched her hands. "I wouldn't have let you risk your hair."

"It's okay," Ashley said again, and Martina thought she sounded annoyed. "I'll live. I'm not that vain."

"But you're a model," Jake said. "Your looks are your life."

Now Ashley was clearly irritated. "I don't mean

to shock you, Jake, but I hope there's a little more to my life than my looks. Especially now."

Then Maura let out another shriek. "Oh no! In all the excitement, Martina forgot to give Cam a haircut!"

"That's okay," Cam said, a little too happily.

Maura gave Ashley one last look of enormous pity. "Thanks, Martina," she chirped, and ran off.

Now everyone was looking at Cam. "What about the tape?" Kesha asked.

"It's major, folks. Let's go to my room."

It wasn't that hard getting away. The so-called Buddies were not really prepared for serious guard duty. Alex had thought that he might have to fight his way out of the hotel. But when he reached the bottom of the stairwell, he could hear the jerk at the door snoring even before he saw him.

He motioned for Shalini to come down and join him, putting a finger to his lips to keep her quiet. He needn't have worried—she was too frightened to speak. He could feel her whole body trembling when he took her hand and led her silently past the Buddy.

Once outside, they walked rapidly for at least ten minutes before he spoke. "You okay?" he asked.

"Yes," she whispered. "Where are we going?"

He didn't have the slightest idea.

twelve

Jake was groggy. He'd been up all night, composing this special edition of the *New World*. He forced himself to give it one last read-through before taking it to the copy shop. The headline wasn't particularly snappy, but he thought it would grab attention.

WHAT REALLY HAPPENED?

A video tape taken from a convenience store surveillance camera offers a new perspective on our situation. Careful analysis of the video frames indicates that there was some sort of presence on earth which caused the disappearance of all people except for this community. In the video, people seem to fade, as if they were being "beamed" away (à la *Star Trek*). As bizarre as this seems, the camera does not lie, and the evidence exists for anyone to see. This video raises serious questions as to the nature of the collapse of our world. More surveillance camera videos must be studied. Community members are urged to collect these tapes from stores and banks and deliver them to Cameron Daley, who will lead the investigation committee.

It wasn't particularly creative, but it got the message across, and that was the important thing. Everyone had to get involved. Of course, there would be skeptics. Jake himself had to scan again and again the enlarged frame photos Cam had brought back from the photo lab. If these photos had appeared in some tabloid newspaper, Jake would have assumed they'd been doctored in some way to make the people appear to be fading. But he trusted Cam, and he knew Cam didn't have that kind of expertise anyway.

He yawned, and looked at the clock. It was almost six in the morning. He wanted to get this thing photocopied and available so that everyone would see it right away. He assumed they'd all want to see the evidence. Maybe he and Cam could set up an exhibit in the hotel lobby. People would get excited. There were so many possibilities, so many implications . . . What had happened to their families, their friends? Was it possible that they were all alive? What should be done, how could they be located, contacted, brought back . . . decisions would have to be made as to how to proceed.

It was overwhelming, and Jake didn't trust his fuzzy mind at the moment. He debated a shower and a change of clothes, but he didn't want to waste one more minute.

There was a Buddy at the door. Carlos was slumped against the wall and yawning. His "halt" wasn't very convincing.

"I'm going over to Kinko's," Jake told him.

"You gotta be accompanied by a Buddy," Carlos said.

"Okay, fine," Jake said hurriedly. "Come on."

"I can't leave my post."

Jake groaned inwardly. These guys were taking themselves way too seriously. He didn't want to start an arguement. "All right, get me another Buddy."

"No one's around, everybody's sleeping."

Jake tried to control his rising annoyance. "Then wake someone up. This is important."

"Yeah? What is it?"

Jake handed him the paper. Carlos read it quickly. Then he read it again. "Is this for real?"

"Yeah."

Carlos bit his lower lip. He read the article again, and he chewed on his lip some more. Jake could see the debate going on in his head.

Then, to Jake's surprise, he pulled a mobile phone from his hip pocket, and dialed some numbers.

"Yeah, I know, sorry to wake you. But I think this is important. Right." To Jake, he said, "You're going to have a wait a minute."

So now he was going to have to wait for some Buddy to get out of bed and dress so he could be accompanied to Kinko's. This game they were playing was getting ridiculous.

It wasn't a Buddy who appeared at the door a few moments later. It was the Head Honcho Himself. It amazed Jake how, at this hour, Travis could still manage to look so pulled together. "What's the problem?" he asked Carlos.

"Robbins wants to go to Kinko's and make copies of this for everyone."

Travis read the article quickly. "Is this some kind of a joke?" he asked Jake.

"No."

"Where is this video now?"

"Cam Daley has it."

Travis nodded slowly. "Jake, you'd better keep this to yourself for a while. I want to think about it."

"What are you talking about?" Jake asked in bewilderment.

"I don't want to throw the community into a panic," Travis said. "We're starting to get organized now, and I think we're moving in the right direction. People are acting civilized, there's law and order. News like this could throw everything into chaos."

Jake was working very hard to keep his impatience from showing. "Look, I know it's pretty shocking. That's why we decided not to run around and bang on people's doors with the news. We're going to present what we've learned this afternoon, here in the lobby, so we can all discuss this rationally."

Travis shook his head. "You can't suddenly give everyone new hope and expect them to behave rationally. It's not the right time, Jake." He crumpled the article in his hand. "I don't want anyone hearing about this. Not yet."

Jake was completely confused. "Then when?"

"Let me think about it," Travis said. He turned and started back toward the stairs.

"Wait a minute," Jake called, running after him. "Travis, what's the matter with you? You can't make this kind of decision for everyone!"

Travis smiled. "I have to, Jake. That's my job."

The words sent a cold chill up Jake's spine. In disbelief, he watched Travis walk away calmly.

He looked at Carlos. Carlos shrugged. "He's the boss."

"Says who?" Jake asked. It was a childish response, but he couldn't think of anything else to say. All Carlos did was shrug again.

Jake considered his options. He wasn't concerned that Jake had taken the article away. He'd written it on his computer, he could print out another copy. But how would he get past Carlos? With physical force?

And now he saw that his obstacle wouldn't be Carlos. The elevator doors opened and Mike Salicki came out. Big, brawny Mike, twice the size of Carlos, and twice as strong as Jake. Mike shot Jake one cold, hard look. Then he joined Carlos at the door.

They didn't have to say anything. Jake knew he wouldn't get past them.

"So what do we do now?" Martina asked.

They were all gathered in her room—Kesha, Cam, Jake, and Ashley. No one had eaten any breakfast yet, and they weren't in the best of moods.

"Donna's gone to talk to Travis," Kesha told them.

"What good will that do?" Jake asked. "I'm telling you, the guy's gone psycho. Why would he listen to Donna?"

"They had a relationship," Kesha said. "Maybe she can connect with him."

It was a brief connection. Donna was back moments later.

"Well?" Jake asked. "Did his goon squad let you get near him?"

Donna nodded, and sat down on Martina's bed.

"So what happened?" Jake pressed.

"Not a whole lot."

"He must have said something," Kesha declared.

"Was he awful to you?" Ashley asked sympathetically.

"No, not awful at all," Donna replied. "Actually, he was kind of sweet."

"Sweet!" Jake was aghast. "How can you call him sweet? He's turning into a dictator!"

"He doesn't know what else to do!" Donna argued. "This hasn't been easy for him, you know. Everyone's expecting him to do what's right for the community. That's a big burden for one person to carry. People want him to take charge."

"Some people," Jake corrected.

"He wants to communicate with everyone," Donna said. "He's called for a meeting of the whole community at noon."

"Oh, great," Jake groaned. "A student council meeting. Just what we need."

Donna was annoyed by his tone. "Look, you don't know Travis. I do. He's no angel, I realize that. He's arrogant and ambitious, and it's true, he thinks he's smarter and better than other people. But he's not evil. He'd never hurt anyone. And look at all the good things he's done! He's practically created a civilization out of twenty-five high school seniors!"

"A civilization that he can rule," Jake muttered. "Well, he can't control what we say. We'll tell everyone about the video at the meeting."

At noon, the lobby was packed. Travis stood by the fireplace again, flanked by his Buddies. "I have something very important to report," Travis announced.

So Travis was going to tell them about their discovery, Martina thought. He'd probably try to take credit for it too.

"Two members of our community, Alex Popov and Shalini Chatterjee, have disappeared." He paused to allow a few gasps and whispers. "We have no idea where they are. They could be anywhere, even out of New York by now. It's impossible to contemplate searching for them." He paused again, and a sorrowful look came over his face. "I don't know how they plan to survive on their own. It saddens me terribly to say this, but I believe they are lost to us."

He paused again, and allowed a few seconds for mourning. Since no one really knew Shalini and practically everyone disliked Alex, they didn't need much more than that.

Now Travis's voice became stronger. "But I'm telling you this, and you must believe me. We will not lose any more members of this community. It simply will not happen. In order to insure this, I have decided that it is necessary to curtail our movements with an increase in surveillance and protective services."

It took a moment for his pompous language to sink in. Then an uneasy murmur went through the room.

"He's done it," Jake whispered to Martina. "He's screwed himself. No one's going to accept this."

Travis held up a hand to stop the noise. "Yes, I know this sounds like I'm imposing some sort of martial law. But you have to understand the essential need for this state of affairs—this temporary state of affairs. Extreme circumstances call for extreme measures. If the services I'm talking about had been in effect yesterday, we would still have Alex and Shalini here with us."

Jake stood up. "I've got something to tell the community."

Travis smiled pleasantly. "Let me finish, Jake, and you'll have a chance to speak. Now, you all must admit that we've been progressing well as a society. No one's starving, everyone's clothed and housed, we have established rules that have made us respect each other. Personally, I think we've done a better job than the society before us."

At that point, the Buddies began to applaud. Martina realized there were more of them than he'd realized, and they weren't all standing up there with Travis. There were red armbands throughout the group sitting around the lobby.

"But we have a long way to go," Travis continued. "A long way, before we can say we have created a true society. Until we feel united as a community, with our goals in consensus, until we have a sincere commitment to the survival, growth, and well-being of the entire community, we must have strict controls."

He went on to elaborate. The controls included compulsory morning roll calls, communal meals, curfews, elaborate procedures for obtaining permission to leave the premises.

Now even one of the Buddies looked alarmed. "We can't go anywhere without permission?" he asked.

"You have complete and free access to the health club across the street," Travis told him. "There will always be a Buddy there."

"The health club?" someone asked. "That's it?"

"Hey, have you been there?" Mike challenged him. "There's an Olympic size indoor pool, a heated outdoor pool on the roof, a jacuzzi, a sauna, a health food bar, a virtual reality gameroom, and even a nightclub with karaoke! There's plenty to keep you happy."

"Geez, he sounds like a prison guard," Martina whispered to Jake.

"That's what he is," Jake replied, and he rose again. "Can I speak now?"

Travis graciously bowed his head and gestured for Jake to come to the fireplace. Jake shook his head.

"I can speak from here. Folks, I have something pretty dramatic to tell you, so prepare yourselves. There is indication that something other than a bomb has removed all the people. And they may not be dead."

A stunned silence greeted this. He half-expected Travis's goons to rush him and drag him from the room, so he kept talking rapidly. He told them about how Martina and Cam had found the video, how they'd studied it at a photo lab, what they'd been able to ascertain.

"We need to see more tapes, and learn all we can. This is just the beginning. But it's pretty exciting, I think."

"How did you treat the photos?" someone asked Martina.

"Cam can answer that better than I can," Martina said. At that moment, she realized that Cam wasn't with them—and that he wasn't in the room at all. "Where is he?"

"Cam is under room arrest," Travis declared calmly.

"What?" Martina thought she was shouting, but the word came out as a frightened whisper.

Travis turned to Mike, and Mike took over. He spoke like a chief of police addressing the press. "Twenty minutes ago, Buddies searched Cam's room. This video tape and some enlarged photographs were taken to be examined. They have proven to be forgeries."

"Forgeries!" Now Martina was able to shout. "Forgeries of what?"

"How should I know?" Mike said. "Ask Cameron Daley, he's the one who made them, he's the one trying to pull off this stupid stunt. I hope he's not considering a career in special effects, because they're not very convincing."

"Wait a minute," Jake cried out. "Why not let the whole group see them and make that decision for themselves?"

"The tape and photographs have been destroyed," Travis said. "Jake, I know that you and Martina were involved in this scam. However, Cam has said that he is primarily responsible, so we have decided that you two will not be arrested."

Kesha rose. "What's the 'we' business? Who's 'we'? Us?"

"As I recall," Travis said, "you people asked me to take over, to get this community organized. Crime and punishment is an aspect of any society. That's all I have to say." He looked at his watch. "Lunch will be at two o'clock in Domino's Restaurant."

No one challenged this. Martina watched in horror as kids chatted about this and that, and drifted out of the room. She turned to Donna.

"You still think he's sweet?"

thirteen

everyone looked up expectantly when Jake came into Martina's room.

"They won't let me see him," Jake told them. "There are two Buddies at his door."

"What about food?" Kesha asked. "He'll starve!"

"Oh no," Donna said quickly. "Travis wouldn't allow something like that to happen."

"They're supposed to bring him meals," Jake said. He pushed hair out of his eyes. He was so exhausted now, he felt like he was functioning on fuel derived from sheer anger. "I don't trust them. We have to get Cam out of there."

"How?" Ashley asked. "There are only five of us."

"That doesn't mean Travis has nineteen on his side," Kesha declared. "There are kids who are just going along with this because they think there's no option."

"We'll give them an option," Jake said grimly. "We have to organize an opposition. We'll make a list of all the people who aren't clearly committed to Travis. We'll divide them up among us, so each of us can talk to one or two privately."

"What will we tell them?" Martina asked.

"To come to a meeting, this afternoon," Jake said. "We could meet at the health club." He turned to Ashley. "You've been there. Where could we have the meeting? Is there an area that's usually deserted?" He tried not to look too pointedly at her bald head. He had to admire her, though. She was doing a good job of pretending she didn't care.

Ashley nodded. "The aerobic classroom on the third floor. There's no equipment up there."

"Okay. We'll tell them to meet there at four. Who should we ask?"

They debated over their classmates. Obviously, anyone wearing a red armband was out. They came up with seven possible candidates. "Don't tell them about the meeting right away," Jake cautioned. "Talk to them first, feel them out, find out what they think about Travis. Then use your best judgment." He parceled out individuals to Kesha, Martina, and Donna. "I'll take care of the rest," he said.

In a deli on the Upper West Side, Alex found some smoked turkey that smelled okay. Shalini gathered a box of crackers, canned peaches, a jar of pickles.

"We're just a couple of blocks from Central Park," Alex said. "Let's eat there."

"All right," Shalini said. "You know, I have never walked in Central Park. My father always forbid me to go there. He said it was a dangerous place. He said many criminals lurk there."

"Not anymore," Alex said. "Besides, you're with me. I won't let anything happen to you."

"I do not feel terribly frightened anymore," Shalini said thoughtfully. "In fact, I feel rather excited."

"Excited? Nothing's happening!"

Shalini smiled. "I am having an adventure. I like this. To walk through Central Park . . . this, for me, is an adventure."

"I'm glad you're seeing it in the fall," Alex said. "It looks great, with the trees and the leaves all different colors. Are you getting tired? We've been walking for almost seven hours."

"I am a bit fatigued," she admitted.

"After lunch, we can go over to the Plaza Hotel. That's a really fancy hotel, much nicer than that dump we've been staying in. We can sleep there." He looked at her anxiously, hoping she wasn't taking that the wrong way. "At least we know there will be plenty of empty rooms," he added hastily.

They'd reached the entrance at 72nd Street. "It's beautiful!" Shalini declared.

"I went to a rock concert here, on the Great Lawn," Alex boasted. "In the summer, it's covered with people, sunbathing, throwing frisbees. Want to see the Great Lawn? Of course, there won't be any people, but it's still cool."

Alex couldn't remember ever appreciating Central Park as much as he did that day. Shalini exclaimed over every tree, every rock, practically every blade of grass. She oohed and ahed each time Alex pointed out a pretty area. She went crazy over Strawberry Fields, the memorial to John Lennon. Alex never would have guessed that a rebel like Lennon would be a hero to someone like Shalini. She was showing new aspects to her personality.

"Now we're getting into the Great Lawn," he told her as they rounded a bend. Then he stopped walking, stood very still, and stared.

"What is that big circle?" Shalini asked. "Some sort of playing field?"

After a few seconds, Alex said, "No. There's no playing field there."

They moved toward the huge, circular, darkened area of the lawn. When they reached the periphery, Shalini bent down and examined the lawn. "The grass looks like it's been in a fire."

Alex knelt down and twisted a blade of grass in his hand. "Yeah. And it's flattened. Like, something was pressing down on it for a while."

"What could make something like this happen?" Shalini wondered. "A fire? A tornado, something like that?"

"I don't know," Alex said. "It looks like . . ." He hesitated, unwilling to say what he was thinking.

Shalini prompted him. "It looks like what?"

"Like something was here."

Martina didn't want to talk to David Chu. She even considered asking Jake to assign David to someone else. But with the current situation, she couldn't go on holding grudges. She had to put her personal feelings aside for a greater good.

She went to David's room and knocked, but there was no response. She knew he could be in almost any girl's room in the building, and she wasn't going to try them all. But no one was going to accuse her of giving up easily. She went to the lobby, and spoke to Adam Wise, the Buddy on duty.

She'd known Adam slightly at school, and used to think he was an okay person. Too bad he was committed to Travis. Still, she tried to smile in a friendly way as she asked him if he knew where David was.

"He's over at the health club," Adam told her.

"Do I need a Buddy to take me over there?"

"Nah," Adam said. "I can watch you from here."

She wondered what was creepier—being accompanied by a guard or knowing you were being watched as you crossed the street. And there was another Buddy standing by the health club door.

Inside, she found David in the weight-lifting room. Fortunately, he was alone.

"Hi," she said.

He grinned. "Wanna spot me?"

She had no idea what that meant. "No." She walked around, and pretended to be interested in examining the equipment. "This is a nice place."

"Not bad," David said. He was hoisting a barbell in front of a mirror, and Martina could see that he was admiring the way his muscles bulged. Conceited creep, she thought.

"Some people were complaining, saying that they'd like more choice in clubs," she said casually.

"Yeah?" David was clearly more interested in his reflection than in making conversation.

"Mm. They think they shouldn't have to take orders about where they can and can't go. How do you feel about that?"

"Okay." David put the weight down, and began flexing in front of the mirror. "Well, I'm not crazy about it. I think Travis is going overboard with this safety stuff. But I can pretty much do what I want."

"But aren't all these rules going to cramp your style?" she pressed. "What about parties? If you're restricted to the hotel and the health club, where are you gonna party?"

"There's plenty of party space here," he said. "And I like having private parties in my room."

"Don't your neighbors complain about the noise?"

"There's not that much noise. Not when it's a party of two." He gave a wicked laugh. "Or three."

He made her sick. "Does it ever bother you?" she asked abruptly. "Going after girls, making them fall in love with you, then dumping them?"

Finally, albeit reluctantly, David turned away from his reflection and actually looked at her. "I don't force them to fall in love. I tell them, let's have fun, let's hang out, that's all."

"Some girls want more than fun," Martina said through clenched teeth. "Like my sister."

"Look," he said. "It's too bad she got so hung up. But you can't blame me. It's not my problem."

An image of Rosa, curled up on her bed, weeping through the night, flashed before Martina's eyes. Rosa, who wasn't around to defend herself.

She hated him. Maybe he could be convinced to join their side. But she didn't want him there. Without another word, she left the room.

fourteen

the huge, darkened area on the Great Lawn wasn't natural at all. Looking at it was giving Alex inexplicable creeps. He didn't want Shalini to see how it was bothering him. She was depending on him, and he had to stay strong, confident, and fearless for her sake.

"Let's get out of here," he said roughly.

But Shalini was fascinated by the crushed grass. She knelt down and touched it. Then she stood up. "I wonder if this is a perfect circle, or simply circular in shape."

"What difference does it make?"

"I'm not sure," Shalini said thoughtfully. "But I'd like to know." She looked toward the tall buildings that faced the park on Fifth Avenue. "We could go to the top of that building and look down on it."

"Why?"

"It would be interesting to see it from another perspective. We might even be able to figure out what it is."

Alex scratched his head. "What's the point?"

Shalini smiled. "Do you have something better to do? Are you perhaps late for an appointment?"

They walked across the park and came out on the Fifth Avenue side. In the tallest building, Shalini pressed a button for the elevator. "I hope the electricity is still working in this part of the city," she said.

"If it's not, you can forget this," Alex said. "No way I'm climbing all these stairs to the top."

But the elevator arrived, and the doors opened. Still, Alex hesitated. "Are you sure you want to do this?" he asked. But Shalini had already walked into the elevator.

"You know, we could lose electricity at any time," he told her. "This elevator could get stuck between floors, and you could press the emergency button forever. There's nobody to rescue us."

She didn't reply. As the elevator moved up, he looked at her curiously. He would have expected a discovery like the one in the park to freak her out. By now, she should be very frightened, huddled in a corner of the elevator, weeping, and he would be comforting her. "Aren't you scared?" he asked cautiously.

"Yes," she said simply. "But this is a very new experience. To be in a mystery. Perhaps just now I am more curious than scared."

Personally, he didn't feel like getting involved in a mystery. But he was still responsible for her. At least, that was how he felt, so he had to go along.

On the top floor of the building, they figured out which room would offer them the best view of the Great Lawn. The door was open, and they went directly to the windows. They stood there, side by side, and looked out.

"It's round," Shalini said. "It is a perfect circle."

"Yeah, so what?"

"It is not a natural phenomenon." She pressed her face against the window. "Do you see the dark lines? They are like rays, coming out from the circle. See? There are four of them."

"Yeah, okay, I see them."

"They are evenly spaced around the circle."

"Yeah, okay, whatever."

"But do you see, Alex? They look as if they could have balanced whatever made the circle. Like some sort of pedestal." After a moment, she added, "Or some sort of landing gear."

Alex turned to her slowly. "Huh?"

"Look at it, Alex," she said insistently. "Some huge, circular object with four things extending from it. What does it look like to you?"

He tried to laugh. "Oh, come on, Shalini. What are you talking about, a flying saucer?"

Shalini smiled. "No, I'm not talking about a flying saucer, Alex. That's only in comic books and silly television shows." She turned back to gaze down on the lawn. "I'm talking about a spacecraft."

Alex didn't know how to respond. All he could manage was, "You have to be kidding."

"You were the one who said it looked like something had been there," she pointed out to him.

"Well, I meant . . . something else, I don't know. Like, like a meteor that fell to earth."

"Where is the meteor now?"

Alex fumbled for another explanation. "Or, or maybe the lawn was struck by lightning. Yeah, that's it. I saw on TV once, this ballpark that was struck by lightning, and it left this big burned spot."

"A spot that formed a perfect circle?"

He fell silent. She was right. There was nothing

natural about that scorched land. "A spacecraft," he said finally. "From another planet?"

She nodded.

"You're talking about Martians?"

"I do not know which planet it came from," Shalini said. "It might not even be from our solar system."

Alex was getting a headache. "I can't get into this," he said. "I don't believe in that crap."

"No, it is not easy to believe in something we have never seen," Shalini acknowledged. "But is it not rather arrogant of us to believe that humans are the only intelligent creatures in the universe?"

What he couldn't believe right now was the fact that she was speaking in a normal tone of voice, that she could speak of spacecraft and Martians and not tremble or cry. Didn't she need him anymore? This timid girl—who had never made a decision, who was afraid of everything—stood here looking at something that could be evidence of some sort of extraterrestrial life form, and she wasn't even nervous. Her eyes were shining.

"Weird," he murmured, and he wasn't sure if he was speaking of the shape on the lawn or her.

"But it is also logical," she said. "Every living body on earth disappears, but there are no bodies, no traces of human remains. So maybe they're not dead, Alex. Maybe they were taken away."

His head was spinning. "Wait a minute. You're saying that some—some aliens came to Earth and took everyone away, except us."

"Perhaps."

"Why not us?"

"We were in the bomb shelter. Maybe they didn't know we were there. Maybe they just missed us."

"That doesn't make sense," Alex said flatly. He grabbed her hand. "Let's get out of here."

"And go where?"

"I don't know. Across the George Washington Bridge, to New Jersey."

"Why should we go there?"

"Well, we can't stay here!" Alex exclaimed. "Whatever was here before—they could come back."

She only heard half of what he said. "No, we can't stay here. We have to go back to the others."

"Are you nuts? Why should we go back there? We just escaped from that place!"

"We have to tell them what we've discovered," Shalini replied.

"Why should we tell those jerks anything?"

"Because they are human beings. We are human beings. We owe it to each other."

"We don't owe them anything," Alex stated. "Let the Martians come back and take them too."

"Oh, no, Alex. If people are going to survive, they have to connect. Remember what you said on the way up here, in the elevator? That if we got stuck, there would be no one to rescue us? We all need to rescue each other."

"Why?" he cried out in frustration. "What's happened to you, Shalini? What's changed?"

She looked out the window at the dark circle. "This," she said simply. "It gives me hope."

Jake was running laps at the health club. Running had always been his way of clearing his head, and getting ideas. Of course, he'd usually had a decent night's sleep before running.

He had to get Cam out of that room. If they were going to form a real opposition to Travis, he needed everyone he could get on his side. And who knew what could happen to Cam, with a maniac like Travis making the rules.

Wild visions ran through his mind. He could organize a team to seek out gun stores, gather weapons, force the guard to release Cam. He wondered if anyone here knew how to use a gun.

Reason took over. If his friends could find weapons, so could the other side. He didn't want a bloodbath.

From just outside the entrance to the track came the sound of giggles. Jake grimaced. What could anyone find to laugh about now?

He couldn't run anymore. He slowed down and went out into the hallway. David Chu, with each of his arms wrapped around a girl, was there. "Yo, Robbins," he called out cheerfully. "Want to join us?"

"What are you doing?" Jake asked.

"We're going into the jacuzzi."

"No thanks," Jake said.

"You won't need a bathing suit," David said, and the two girls started giggling again. They moved on toward the door which led to the pool and the jacuzzi. Even after they'd disappeared from view, Jake could still hear them laughing.

Jake tried to recall the names of the two girls who'd been hanging onto David. Courtney, that was one of them. The other one was Michelle or Nicole or something like that. Both seemed pretty vacant. He'd never paid any attention to either of them back at school.

But he supposed that for someone like David, any girl was worth pursuing, if only for a brief fling. It didn't matter if she was intelligent, if she had personality, if she was pretty, as long as she was female. Jake could never relate to that attitude about women, but he supposed there were a lot of guys who felt that way. If any girl behaved in a mildly provocative way, they were ready to jump her bones . . .

That was when the idea hit him—the way to get Cam out of his room. It was so clear, so obvious, he was appalled that it hadn't occurred to him sooner. Lack of sleep had taken its toll.

He didn't even take the time to shower. He ran to the weight room, where he knew Ashley was working out.

Ashley didn't see him come in. She was lifting some small hand weights in front of a mirror. Beads of sweat dotted her forehead. She wore a tight leotard and tiny shorts, and even with her bald head, she looked unbelievably sexy.

There was no way this couldn't work. He came up behind her. She smiled at his reflection in the mirror. "I'm working off tension," she said. "I want to be in good shape for that meeting. I have a feeling we may be forming an army."

"I had an idea," he said abruptly. "How to rescue Cam."

"Yeah?"

"I need your help. It's the perfect job for you."

She put the weights down. "What's your idea?"

"Let's go back to the hotel. I'll tell you on the way."

She nodded. "Just let me change my clothes."

"There's no time for that," Jake said. "Come on."

She must have heard the urgency in his voice, because she didn't argue. She grabbed a towel to wipe the sweat from her brow, and together they left the club.

"Now, tell me what's going on," she said as they crossed the street.

"I need you to distract the guard at Cam's door so I can get Cam out."

She was puzzled. "Good grief, Jake, even if I can get him to look the other way for a moment, he's still going to know if you go into Cam's room."

"He won't know if he's not there," Jake said. "You're going to get him to leave his post."

As they entered the hotel, Scott Spivey was guarding the door, and he leered at the sight of Ashley's scantily-clad body. "Having fun?" he asked, wriggling his eyebrows up and down.

Ashley gave him a withering look, but Jake was secretly pleased. This was more evidence that his plan would work.

They took the stairs up to the floor where Cam was being held. From the stairwell, they peered around the corner, and focused on the guard in front of Cam's room.

"Good," Jake said. "It's Andy."

"Why is that good?"

"Because he's a sex maniac. Or he likes to think he is. And he thinks you're great-looking. At least, he used to, when you had hair."

"What does that have to do with anything?"

"That's how you're going to get him away from the door," Jake told her. "You'll go over there, without me, and flirt with him."

There was no expression on Ashley's face. "I will?"

"Yes. Say whatever you can think of, that you've been dreaming about him, that you've got the hots for him, something like that. I don't think you'll have to be subtle. He'll try to make a date to meet you later, but you tell him you have to have him now, right this minute, while you're in the mood. There's a vacant room at the far end of the hall. You can take him in there."

His mind was racing feverishly as he worked out all possible problems. "Tell him he won't be going far, and he'll be able to hear anything happening in the hall. Only he won't, because you'll put on music, or make a lot of noise or something. By then, he won't care, he'll be so turned on."

"And then?"

Was it his imagination, or had her voice suddenly gone flat?

"Get him to take his clothes off first. Then, say you need to get something from your room. A condom. If he doesn't want you to leave, just make a dash for it. He won't run out of the room naked. By the time he gets his clothes back on, you'll be back at the health club. And so will Cam and me. Okay? Got it?"

She didn't answer.

"Got it?" he asked again.

"I get it," she said, and now he could actually feel the coldness in her voice. "You think this is the only way I can assist you, the only purpose I can serve. I can use my body and my looks. Because that's all I am to you, a face and a body. You're not interested in my brain, you're not even considering the possibility that I might have the intelligence to come up with a plan of my own."

"Ashley, we don't have time for a feminist argument!" He said testily.

She continued as if he hadn't spoken. "That's why you were so upset about my hair. You thought it might make me less appealing, and I wouldn't have as much power as a sex object. You were afraid you wouldn't be able to dangle me as bait in front of other guys."

"That's crazy!" Jake declared.

"No, I'm crazy," she retorted. "Crazy for thinking you were any different from every other macho creep." With that, she turned around and ran down the stairs.

"Ashley, wait!"

But she was gone.

Fury rose up inside him. A frustration, an anger, a rage he'd never known before was burning in his gut. He was not going back to that health club without Cam. He came out into the hallway. If he had to slug it out with Andy, so be it.

"What do you want?" Andy asked.

Jake opened his mouth, but before any words could come out, he felt a hand clamp down on his shoulder. He turned.

"Hi, Jake." Adam Wise grinned at him, and then spoke to Andy. "You can take off, man. I'm here to relieve you."

"Okay." Andy jerked his head toward Jake. "Keep an eye on this guy."

"Right," Adam said. "Hey, there's a poker game in Salicki's room. They're looking for a fourth."

"Gotcha," Andy said.

As soon as he disappeared, so did Adam's grin. "Come on," he said to Jake. "We have to work fast."

Jake looked at him. "What are you talking about?"

"You want to get Daley out of here, don't you?"

He didn't wait for Jake to confirm that. He opened the door, but Jake held back. Was Adam planning to push him in there, and take him as an additional prisoner?

But Adam went into the room first. "C'mon, let's go," he said to Cam.

Cam looked wary. Then he saw Jake just behind Adam. He rose from his chair and came out of the room.

"We don't have much time," Adam said. "There's no poker game in Salicki's room." He started down the hall, with a hand gripping Cam's arm. Jake followed them down the stairs. Scott Spivey was still at the main door. He looked at Cam, and then at Adam. "What's going on?"

"The prisoner has to get some exercise," Adam said.

Scott gave Cam's scrawny body a once-over. "He can use it. What's he doing with you?" he asked, looking suspiciously at Jake.

"I'm not with them," Jake retorted. "I'm just going over to the health club. That's still allowed, right?"

"So far," Scott said.

Jake kept some distance behind Adam and Cam as they crossed the street, in case Scott was watching. But inside the health club, Jake led them to the aerobics room. Martina, Kesha, and Donna were already there.

"Cam!" Martina shrieked. She leaped up, ran over and threw her arms around him. Cam turned red, but he didn't push her away.

"Are you okay?" Kesha asked. "What did they do to you?"

"I'm okay, and nobody did anything to me," Cam told them. "They brought me food, and Adam here picked up videos for me."

"See?" Donna said to the others. "I told you Travis wouldn't let anyone hurt him."

"Did Ashley come back here?" Jake asked.

No one had seen her. He figured she was probably sulking in another part of the club. He'd go look for her in a minute and set things straight.

"What are you doing here?" Kesha asked Adam. "Aren't you a Buddy?"

"I was," Adam said. He pulled off the red armband. "I don't like what's going on. And I know you guys are starting up some kind of rebel group."

"How did you know that?" Jake asked suspiciously. Adam hadn't been on their list of possible supporters.

Adam cocked his head toward Cam. "He told me."

"Cam!" Martina was appalled. "You told a Buddy about us?"

"Yeah," Cam said. "We got to talking about dictators and totalitarian governments and all that. I could tell he was okay."

"He told me about the cassette Martina found in the classroom, and the security tape. I'm with you."

Jake nodded his approval. "Who else can we expect?"

As it turned out, no one had managed to identify another potential rebel. Some people were too scared. Others didn't care.

So they were only seven, and one of the seven was missing. "I'm going to find Ashley," Jake said.

But he couldn't. He explored every area of the huge health club, from the karaoke room to the tanning salon, but he couldn't locate her. Maybe she was sulking back in her room at the hotel. He could go back there and try to apologize.

He headed back to the aerobics room to tell them he was running out for a minute. But as he approached the room, he heard raised voices. He quickened his step and went in.

Scott Spivey was there. "Nobody authorized any exercise for Daley," he announced. "I'm supposed to take him back to his room." He turned to Adam. "And you're in big trouble. Mike says he's going to take your armband."

"He can't," Adam said. "It's already gone."

Scott's brow furrowed. "What's going on here?"

"We're having a meeting," Jake said.

"What kind of a meeting?"

"None of your business."

"Maybe I can make it my business."

"There's six of us against one of you, Spivey," Jake pointed out.

Scott pulled the mobile phone from his pocket. "Yeah, well, all I have to do is make a call and I'll have at least half a dozen Buddies over here to help me out."

It was incredible, how an overtired mind could somehow rise to the occasion. Jake knew what to do. "Go ahead and call," he said.

Fortunately, Scott wasn't a mental giant. As soon as he finished punching in the numbers, Jake moved like lightning. He managed to get the phone away from Scott. Of course, Scott came after him, but Kesha and Adam pulled him back.

He didn't recognize the voice that answered. "I want to talk to Travis."

"Who is this?"

"Get Travis."

"Is that you, Robbins?"

By then, Jake knew who he was talking to. "Look, Salicki, just put Travis on."

"Why?"

"Because I want to organize a meeting with him. Now."

"Okay," Mike said. "Come on down to the lobby and Travis will meet with you."

"No," Jake said. "Not at the hotel. Here, at the health club."

"Sorry, man," Mike said easily. "No way."

Jake held the phone toward Scott. "Say hello, Scott."

Scott didn't speak. But Kesha pinched him roughly in the gut, and he let out a yelp.

"Did you hear that?" Jake asked into the phone. "We have your friend Spivey. And he's staying here, until we get a meeting with Travis."

There was a pause, and he could hear Mike whispering to someone else. Then he was back on the phone. "And if I say no? I got a lot of friends here, Robbins. We could take the health club, easy."

"And what's going to happen to Spivey?" Jake said.

"Oh, come on, you saying you're holding him hostage? What are you going to do to him?"

Jake didn't have the slightest idea, but he made his voice sound as threatening as possible. "You don't want to know."

There was a click on the other end, and the line was disconnected. "Lock all the doors," Jake ordered Donna.

Martina and Cam located some jump ropes in an exercise room. Having been Boy Scouts, both Cam and Jake knew how to make some serious knots. They tied Spivey's arms together, and walked him downstairs to the health bar, where they could watch the hotel from the window. Then they tied his legs together, pushed him into a chair and tied a rope around him.

"Now what?" Donna asked Jake.

"Now, we wait."

And wait they did, for what felt like an hour. Apparently, Travis or Mike or somebody had decided against storming the health club.

"How long can we stay here, without food?" Donna wondered.

Martina was examining the health bar. "There's juice and granola bars back here. Dried fruit and nuts, too. That'll keep us going for a while."

"Not forever," Spivey spat out. "And as soon as any one of you tries to leave, they'll get you."

The mobile phone rang. "Yeah?" Jake barked.

"Jake, this is Travis." His voice was calm and smooth.

"We have to talk," Jake said.

"Yes, I realize that," Travis said. "But you won't come here to meet with me."

"That's right," Jake said. "You have to come here. Alone, without your bodyguards."

"And how do I know you won't take me hostage too?" Travis asked.

He had a point.

"I have a proposition," Travis continued. "Release Spivey. Then I'll know you can be trusted, and we'll arrange a mutually satisfactory meeting."

Spivey was their only bargaining unit. "No," Jake said.

Travis sighed. "Jake, get real. You've got what, six people there? We could storm the health club and drag you all out."

"We're watching the door," Jake said. "One of

you steps out of the hotel, you can forget about Spivey."

Travis's voice was silky. "And do you really think we care that much about Spivey?"

Jake's heart stood still. Maybe those fascists really were cold enough to sacrifice Spivey. "I've got another proposition," he said. "We'll send you Spivey, you send us . . . Ashley."

He could hear whispers again, and then Travis spoke. "All right. You send Spivey over here, and we'll tell Ashley she can go to you."

"No, we exchange at the same time," Jake said. "I can see the front door of the hotel from where I'm standing. When I see Ashley outside, I'll let Spivey out."

"Agreed," Travis said. He hung up.

Todd kept an eye on Spivey while the rest of them went to the window. It was dark out now, but eventually, they made out the figure of a girl stepping out the front door of the residence.

"It's her," Martina said. "It's Ashley."

"Okay," Jake said. He turned to Cam and nodded. Cam cut the ropes that bound Spivey, and Spivey staggered to the door. Kesha opened it and let him out.

Jake kept his eyes on the figure across the road. "Why isn't Ashley moving?" he asked.

"Maybe they won't let her cross the street until they see Spivey," Martina said. But now Spivey was on the street, crossing to the other side. He was moving right under a street light. There was no way Ashley, or anyone else watching, couldn't see him coming.

"Come on, Ashley," Jake muttered urgently. "Get moving!"

Now Spivey was climbing the steps to the hotel.

And Jake watched in horror as Ashley opened the door for him, and then went back into the hotel behind him.

"Ohmigod," Kesha whispered. "They must have threatened her. Maybe someone was holding a gun on her!"

"It was a trick!" Martina cried out. "We were betrayed!"

They all turned toward Jake, questions in their eyes, waiting for him to tell them what they should do next. He'd never felt such responsibility in his life. And he could only think of one thing to say.

"It's war."

fifteen

as they turned off Sixth Avenue onto the street, Alex couldn't exactly say he was having second thoughts—this was more like his eighty-second thought. He could see the hotel now, and it seemed to be emanating bad vibrations. Flashes of red armbanded pseudo-cops crossed before his eyes. The place was full of animals, and Travis was king of the jungle. Why was he voluntarily going back?

He glanced at Shalini, walking by his side. Her steps had slowed, too. The gleam in her eyes was fading. She was getting that frightened look again.

"You don't want to go back there either," he said.

She was silent, and then she said, "We have no choice. They have to know about this."

"And if they don't believe us?"

"We have the photos, remember?"

That had been Shalini's idea. Back uptown, they'd left the high-rise and located a camera store. They'd taken the best instant photo camera they could find, then they'd gone back to the top of that building and photographed the dark circle. The results weren't super sharp, but they were clear enough to see something on the Great Lawn that shouldn't be there.

As slowly as they were walking, they were still getting closer and closer, and even in the darkness, Alex could see someone with a red armband just outside the door. He gripped Shalini's hand and pulled her behind a car, out of viewing range of the person at the door.

"Let's think about this," he pleaded with her.

She didn't argue, but her voice was full of despair. "We can't stay out here forever, Alex!"

Adam looked. He didn't see any Buddies in front of the health club. He nudged Shalini. "Come on," he said, grabbing her hand. "Run!"

He didn't dare look back as they raced across to the health club, but he didn't hear any footsteps behind them. His heart almost stopped when he saw that the lobby of the health club was dark— had it been closed and locked? But no, when he pushed on the door it gave way, and they were inside.

"You okay?" he asked Shalini.

She didn't get a chance to respond—only to gasp as she was pulled away from him. Then he felt strong hands pull his own arms back, and he was helpless.

The lights went on. He recognized Kesha holding Shalini. "Let her go!" he bellowed as he tried to pull free from his own captor. He couldn't budge.

"It's Alex and Shalini," he heard someone say. "Where have you guys been?"

"None of your damned business," Alex snarled.

Jake appeared in front of him. He nodded. The grip on Alex's arms was loosened. Turning, Alex recognized the guy—Adam, one of the Buddies.

Adam must have watched a lot of cop shows on TV. He did an expert job patting Alex down. Meanwhile, Kesha was going through Shalini's bag, and found the photos.

"What are these?"

"Don't answer that," Alex told Shalini.

Jake looked over Kesha's shoulder. "Did you take these photos?"

"Yes," Shalini said.

"Shalini!"

"Alex, we have to tell them. We can't do anything by ourselves." She told them about their discovery in Central Park. Others gathered around to examine the photos, and Alex could tell from their faces that the pictures were making an impact. Shalini didn't even have to tell them about the conclusions they'd drawn.

"It has to be some sort of transportation," Cam said, and no one tried to argue with him.

"And everyone's been transported," Martina whispered.

Kesha, ever the skeptic, had to take issue with that. "Oh, come on. The entire population of the earth couldn't fit on something that size. The population of New York wouldn't fit!"

"It's possible," Cam said, "if they were reduced in some way. To a microscopic size. Or if there were other ships."

Kesha gave up.

Jake described their situation to Shalini and Alex. Alex wasn't impressed. "And there's what—six of you against the rest of them?"

"It's a start," Adam said. "We'll get more. People will defect."

"Or you'll take them hostage," Alex said. "Like us."

"No one's a hostage," Jake said. "You can go. But we're keeping these photos. They'll just destroy them over there."

"Maybe not," Donna said. "Maybe this will convince Travis that something did happen. Then we can all be united, and start working together."

Adam didn't like that idea. "No, Travis has a lot of pride. He'll never admit he was wrong."

"He'll have to," Cam insisted. "We've got evidence."

But Martina, too, had doubts. "Even if Travis does believe those photos are real, he won't want to give up his leadership."

"Why should he give it up?" Donna wanted to know. "He's organized, he's intelligent, people look up to him . . ."

"He's also an egotistical tyrant who's let power go to his head," Kesha stated.

"What do you think?" Cam asked Jake.

Jake spoke carefully. "I want to call Travis and tell him about this. I want to try again to have a meeting with him. Donna's right, he is intelligent, and maybe he will believe these pictures."

Alex gave an ugly laugh. "So you're making the decisions for this group, huh? You're just another egotistical tyrant."

"I don't make the decisions," Jake said. "But I can call for a vote. Everyone in favor of contacting Travis, say 'aye.' "

There was a chorus of "ayes." Jake turned to Shalini and Alex. "You can vote too."

"Aye," Shalini said softly.

Kesha and Alex voted "Nay." But Kesha just said, "Majority rules."

"So now I'm trapped here," Alex said.

"No, you're not trapped," Jake said. "You can leave anytime you want."

Alex shrugged. "I'll hang around for a while. For Shalini. To make sure none of you goons hurt her."

Jake nodded. "Will you all trust me to negotiate with Travis?"

There was a general bobbing of heads. Jake took the mobile phone and dialed. He spoke quietly, for a very brief time.

"He's coming."

"Alone?" Adam asked.

"No, he refused to come alone."

"Great," Alex sneered. "He'll come over with his Buddies and take over."

Jake shook his head. "I told him one bodyguard, that's all."

But Travis came with two, Mike and David Chu, who had apparently joined the Buddies and was now wearing a red armband. Jake faced him through the door's window, and held up one finger. Mike pressed a note against the glass, Jake read it aloud. " 'I will remain outside, to alert the others if you take Travis hostage.' "

Kesha sniffed. "Travis doesn't take any chances, does he?" There was a grudging admiration in her voice.

Martina let out a short laugh. "What kind of bodyguard is David Chu? He's a lover, not a fighter."

Jake let Travis and David inside. Alex couldn't help noticing the difference in the two so-called leaders. Jake was looking pretty cruddy, like he hadn't showered or shaved or changed his clothes in a while. Travis, on the other hand, looked like a diplomat. They sat down at a table, facing each other.

"We have evidence," Jake told Travis, "of an extraterrestrial visit that may account for the disappearance of life on this planet. We believe there is a possibility that everyone was abducted. You've seen the video, and you heard the cassette Martina had. I think you should accept this evidence."

Travis looked at the photos. He showed them to David, who looked fascinated. Then he gave the photos back to Jake. "It's a hoax," he said.

Shalini gasped. "I took those pictures myself!"

Travis turned to her. "I'm not accusing you, Shalini. But there could be other explanations."

"Such as?" Jake asked.

Travis took back a photo and studied it. "All right, here's a possibility. The sun moved closer to the earth, or the earth to the sun. All life forms were burned and disintegrated. We alone survived because the sun's rays couldn't penetrate the bomb shelter."

"And the dark circle?" Jake asked.

"Scorched earth," Travis said. "There are probably burn marks like this all over the world."

"Oh, puh-leeze," Kesha said. "That is so lame, Travis."

"I suppose it's a possibility," Jake said slowly. "But Travis, why not let the whole community see these photos. Let them decide what they mean."

Travis shook his head. "It would only create hysteria, mass panic. We're starting to function pretty well now. I don't want anything to disrupt the community."

"Don't you think they're entitled to know about this?" Jake asked.

Travis shook his head. "You have to understand. They are all like children now, frightened and uncertain. They want order, protection. Too many new ideas . . . this would only frighten them."

Jake spoke earnestly. "We're all frightened, Travis. But don't you think we'd be feeling more brave if we were all together, united? And seeking the truth?"

Travis became pensive. "I want us to be united. We all do. We want you guys to come back to the hotel."

"Fat chance," Kesha said.

Travis continued as if she hadn't spoken. "There will be no retribution, no punishment for your rebellion. I give you my word of honor. We could form a coalition government, and work on a constitution together. We could have elections."

"And the photos?" Jake asked.

"No," Travis said. "It's too soon; people aren't ready."

"Then I can't agree," Jake said. "Either we show everyone the photos today, or we stay here. And we form an alternative community."

Travis looked around. "I'm pleading with you," he said. "Come back. We're all that's left in the world, we need each other. Please."

What a cornball, Alex thought. He couldn't believe that Donna was actually crying.

"Anyone here who wants to go back to the hotel can go," Jake said. But nobody did. Travis sighed, and began to rise.

Alex moved swiftly. Before Travis was standing erect, he was behind him. One hand was on a shoulder, pushing Travis back down. The other hand whipped a knife out of his pocket and held it to Travis's throat.

Jake leaped up. "Alex! What the hell do you think you're doing?"

Alex ignored him, and spoke to Travis. "You're going to get on the phone right now and tell your community to come outside. They're going to see these photos now."

Travis somehow maintained a calm voice. "I can't make a phone call with a knife at my throat."

"You make the call," Alex ordered David.

David looked uneasy. "Hey, man, I don't want to get involved."

"What do you mean you don't want to get involved?" Alex exclaimed. "You're his bodyguard!"

"It doesn't matter," Travis said. "No one is making any calls."

"You'd rather die?" Alex asked.

Martina sidled over to Jake. "We could keep him as a hostage," she said. "For Ashley."

"Actually, I have a message for you from Ashley," Travis said. "It's in my jacket pocket."

Alex reached into the pocket and pulled out a folded paper. He tossed it to Jake. Jake opened it and read silently. Then he tossed it to the floor.

Martina picked up the note and read it aloud. " 'Dear Jake, I am not being held hostage. I have decided to stay here, with the community. You have no real need for me, not in the way I want to be needed. Maybe I can use my brain here. Please don't try to bring me back. Ashley.' Is it her handwriting, Jake?"

Jake nodded.

"Someone forced her to write that," Kesha declared.

"No," Jake said. "They're her words. Let Travis go, Alex."

"What?"

"Drop the knife, let him go. No violence. That's not how this group is going to operate."

Incredulous, speechless, Alex didn't move. But when Cam reached over and took the knife from his hand, he didn't resist.

Still maintaining his dignity, Travis rose. "We're free to go?"

"Yes," Jake said.

"Come on, David."

But David didn't move. "Uh, no offense, Travis. But I think I'll stay here."

"Why?" Travis asked.

"I don't know. They just seem like a more fun bunch." He grinned. "Maybe we can party down with the aliens."

Travis didn't argue with him. He nodded, and started out of the health club.

"Wait!" Donna cried out.

Travis stopped and looked back. "What?"

"I'm coming with you," Donna said.

"Donna!" Jake exclaimed. At the same time, Kesha cried out, "Donna!" and her tone was anguished.

Travis smiled. He held out his hand, and Donna took it. They left together.

Alex wouldn't have thought a tough chick like Kesha could cry. But she was crying now. The others looked stunned.

Martina spoke. "What will we do now?"

They all looked at Jake, waiting for an answer.

"Don't look at me," Jake said. "Look at us. That's what our new world is going to be about."

epilogue

"**do we call** this a cease-fire?" Martina asked.

"I'm not sure," Jake said. "If there hasn't been any firing, how can there be a cease-fire?"

"So what do we call it? Detente? A temporary halt to hostilities? Peace?"

They were sitting on the terrace of the outdoor pool, looking up at the night sky. It had been two days since they met with Travis. Across the street, a banner had been strung between the far windows on the top floor of the hotel. It read: THE COMMUNITY.

They hadn't put up a banner at the health club. They weren't staying. They'd voted unanimously, that morning, to leave the club and head uptown to Central Park. Since that was where the alien ship had landed, they'd figured that would be the best place to make contact with whoever, whatever, was on that ship.

Martina had voted with the rest of them, of course. But she couldn't ignore the nagging fears in her head.

"Jake . . ."

"Hm?"

"What if . . ."

"What if what?"

"Well, what if someone gets sick, or breaks a leg, or gets pregnant? I don't trust David around any female. And what if—"

Jake cut in. "What if aliens landed on earth and took all the people away?"

Martina had to smile. "Okay. I get your point." After a moment, she said, "I had a dream last night. About my sister, Rosa."

"Oh yeah?"

"Maybe it wasn't a dream." She glanced at him, and the lack of skepticism on his face encouraged her to continue. "She's alive; I know she's alive. She's glad we're not giving up, that we're going to search for her, and everyone."

Jake said nothing.

"Do you think I just imagined that?" she asked.

"Not necessarily," he said. "Hope is going to be what keeps us going."

He didn't sound particularly hopeful at that moment. Martina looked at him with sympathy. "You miss Ashley, don't you?"

"Yes."

She tried to think of something optimistic to say. "Well, you never know what could happen. Maybe someday . . ."

He looked at her. "Yeah, maybe someday." Then he returned his gaze to the stars. "And it's not as if it was the end of the world."

*Will the kids from Madison High
solve the disappearance
or are they doomed to remain
the Last On Earth?
Don't miss the next exciting installment:*

LAST ON EARTH #2: THE CONVERGENCE

*Coming in December 1998
from Avon Books*

the harlem streets were completely, utterly silent. Even on 125th Street, once a major thoroughfare, Kesha could hear her own footsteps. She took her time, absorbing the atmosphere. It had been a while since Kesha had been uptown in the old neighborhood. Four weeks, at least. Since the day of the Disappearance.

She was coming up to her old elementary school now, and she paused to peer through the wire fence at the playground. She pictured herself there at age eight, her hair gathered in a dozen neat braids, each one punctuated with a color ribbon to match whatever sweater she was wearing. Friends from childhood often told her she dressed better then than she did now, at age seventeen. That was because her mother was in charge back then, and she wouldn't let Kesha out of the house until she was fit to be on the cover of Vogue, kiddie version. If Mama could see her now, in her beat-up baggy overalls, a jersey with a hole at one elbow, her dark curls pulled back messily with a band, she'd have a fit. But Mama wasn't going to see her now, so Kesha had nothing to worry about.

She moved on, past the coffee shop where Daddy

used to take her and her brothers for hot fudge sundaes on special occasions. She passed Hauser's Shoes, where old Mr. Hauser had fit her for a new pair of patent leather Mary Janes every Easter. She passed the corner where the boys used to hang out with their boom boxes, chanting along with their favorite rap songs. Across the street was the church where one of her brothers had sung in the choir.

Then she turned onto the street she had called home.

So many people, even some of her friends, had a false perception of Harlem. They saw it as a land of drug dealers, drive-by shootings, and gang wars. They didn't know about streets like this one, lined with leafy trees and beautifully restored historic homes which reflected the pride of their owners. Kesha had lived in one of those houses with her mother and father, her two older brothers, and her grandmother.

She walked up the steps of the stoop where she used to sit licking a popsicle on hot summer nights. With her hand on the doorknob, she hesitated. She took a deep breath and walked in.

Waves of memory washed over her and suddenly her eyes were stinging. The scent of the potpourri her grandmother loved was still in the air. Hurrying up the stairs, she went directly to her old bedroom.

She dug out an old knapsack from the back of her closet and began to stuff it with the items she'd come here for—books, including her prized Maya Angelou poetry collection, autographed by the poet herself; some framed family photos; the watch that had been her sixteenth birthday present; a favorite sweatshirt; a couple of flannel nightgowns; her old broken-in hiking boots.

She didn't really *need* those hiking boots. There were brand-new ones in her closet downtown. She had gotten them a few weeks ago at Bloomingdale's, where she and Donna and Martina had gone on a shopping spree. She remembered how strange it had been back then, walking out of a department store with items they hadn't purchased. They'd felt like shoplifters. But there was no one to pay, so they didn't have any choice. Of course, she didn't feel strange about it anymore. No one did. They were accustomed to taking what they wanted, when they wanted it, at whatever store happened to be convenient.

No, she didn't need her old boots. But if anyone asked why she'd gone home, she could say it was because there was nothing like old broken-in boots, and it would be ages before the new ones would be that comfortable. And since she was here, she might as well grab some personal mementos. There were some things a person couldn't find in a department store. But the boots provided her with a good excuse, so no one would suspect she'd gone suddenly sentimental.

Once the knapsack was full, she zipped it up, threw it over her shoulder and ran downstairs and out the door. Outside, she walked briskly, trying not to think about the total absence of life around her. Sometimes she felt like she could almost *hear* the silence.

She tried not to look at the houses that stood empty, waiting to be lived in again. There was a motorcycle parked in front of one of them, and she considered taking it back downtown. But it was a cool autumn day, a nice day for a walk. Besides, she was in no rush to get back there. She would only become more and more frustrated watching the others do nothing.

And they called themselves rebels—hah! Jake Robbins spent his days alone—jogging, swimming, working out—and for what? Not in preparation for battle with the community, that was for sure. Jake wasn't the warrior type. He probably just wanted to look good when and if his girlfriend, ex-super model Ashley Silver, ever came back to him. Kesha wanted to tell him not to hold his breath. Ashley would never leave the comfort of private rooms in a nice hotel for a futon on the floor of a health club.

And Kesha's pal, Martina Santiago, who had been full of spirit just a week ago, now spent her time alone, moping, probably in delayed mourning for the loss of her identical twin sister. That was sad, of course, but they'd all lost families and friends. Moping wouldn't bring anyone back.

What kind of rebels spent their days in isolation, not communicating, caught up in their own little worlds? Maybe she wasn't being fair. Some people needed the safety and security of something they could call a home. They were still in a state of shock. One month ago, twenty-five seniors from Madison High School had emerged from an underground classroom to find that every other person on earth had vanished.

What Kesha wanted to say to all of them was this: Get over it! It was time to shake off the shock and the fear and the sadness and move on. They'd had a month to deal with it, wasn't that enough?

A month . . . now that was hard even for Kesha to grasp. Sometimes it seemed like yesterday. Other times she felt as if it had been many months, years even, since D-day.

That's what they called it now, D-day, for lack of a better word. Some thought the D stood for death. Kesha's group believed it meant disappearance.

Kesha turned off 125th Street, and now she was heading down Amsterdam Avenue. Her pace slowed as she walked through the campus of Columbia University, with its trees and grass and stately buildings. The silence here seemed more normal. This could be a semester break, when the students were away. Or she could pretend this was exam week, and everyone was in the library studying.

She'd hoped to be a freshman here next fall. Her grades were high, and if she did well enough on her SATs, she'd have a good chance of getting in. Her parents would have wanted her to live at home and commute, but she'd been wondering if it wouldn't be more fun to live in the dorm . . .

She shook her head vigorously, as if the action would knock these foolish thoughts out of her mind. Universities, dorms, SATs . . . these things had no place in their world today.

Or maybe she should say, their two worlds. After D-day, they'd begun their new life together, all twenty-five of them. In a small Soho hotel, they'd settled down and called themselves the community. Former senior class president Travis Darrow had taken over, with their blessing.

Well, most of them gave their blessing. Kesha didn't think much of Travis. Some people might assume they would have a relationship of some sort, since they were the only African-Americans to survive the Disappearance. But that common denominator didn't bring them any closer together. And the fact that Travis had beat her out in the election for senior class president certainly didn't help.

As far as Kesha was concerned, Travis was nothing more than a would-be politician, with all the flaws that role implied. He came from a political family—in fact, his father was one of the most influential African-Americans in government. Travis looked good, in a well-groomed preppy way. He spoke well, and he had the kind of confidence that came from growing up surrounded by wealth and important people. Travis was a class act, Kesha had to acknowledge that. She had to admit that he had charisma, and all those years in bureaucratic school politics had left him with some real organizational skills. But in Kesha's opinion, that smooth, confident, in-charge exterior was just a facade. Her own observations of Travis had led her to believe that he was actually an insecure mess, and power was the only thing that made him feel good about himself.

Travis had goals. "We are the world," he said. "We're all that's left. We have to get over our grief and accept that. And in the memory of those who are gone, we have to recreate a civilization."

Kesha thought she knew why Travis didn't want them to grieve too much. Grief could lead to anger, which could lead to action. He didn't want any investigation of the situation, any disruption of the status quo. He had a nice little world now, that he could take over and control. If everyone would put their faith in him, he could direct the creation of a new society.

But not everyone could function easily in Travis's rigid society. There were too many rules and regulations, committees, assigned duties and responsibilities, curfews, that sort of thing. On top of that, not everyone could accept what had happened.

Kesha and some others who were dissatisfied with the state of things had turned to Jake for help. For the life of her, Kesha couldn't remember *why* they'd chosen Jake. Sure, he was a nice guy. He was good-looking, too, in a low-key way, with strong features and warm brown eyes. He wrote sensitive editorials for the school paper, and he'd written a couple of poems for the school literary magazine. He didn't have what could be called a magnetic personality, and he certainly wasn't the life of any party, but he had a deliberate, thoughtful air that inspired trust. He seemed like someone who wouldn't freak out easily.

Jake had led the so-called rebels to a new home, a health club just across the street from the hotel. It was supposed to be a temporary stop, giving them a moment to catch their collective breath, and giving the others a chance to join them. Then they were to take off, in search of—what? Answers. Answers to questions like: Why had it happened? Who made it happen? Why were twenty-five high school seniors the only people left on earth? Where was everyone else?

But it had been a week now since the rebels had left the community, and they were still living much as they had before, only without the amenities of private hotel rooms. Of course, Jake hadn't tried to establish the kinds of rules and regulations that Travis had imposed. Jake had done nothing at all. His air of quiet deliberation had given way to something that resembled sleepwalking. Everyone was doing his or her own thing, which was better than following Travis's rules, but it was getting them nowhere.

At 86th Street, Kesha turned east. A few minutes of walking brought her to Central Park. There amidst acres of meadows, lakes, fountains and playgrounds, she realized that this was where they should all be right now. Not huddled together in a pseudo-society, or living as totally unconnected individuals.

Maybe unconnected wasn't the right word. The rebels spoke to each other. They said "hi" and "let's get something to eat" stuff like that. Sometimes they watched videos together on the bigscreen TV in the lounge, and critiqued them afterward. But that was about it. They didn't talk about anything meaningful, anything real. They weren't bonding.

At least, most of them weren't bonding. Alex and Shalini, two misfits, had connected in a very weird way. What a pair they made—the quiet, mousy little Indian girl and the angry, sullen boy who looked like he was born in a leather jacket. The least communal of the group, they'd been the first to leave the community. But they'd returned, with a revelation.

Kesha walked through Central Park along the 86th Street Transverse Road. That led her directly onto the vast expanse of green known as the Great Lawn, where she could look for herself at what she'd only seen in the photographs Alex and Shalini had brought back with them.

It was a huge, darkened area of crushed grass, still plainly visible after a month. Something very large and round had been there. The photos were taken from one of the highrise buildings on Fifth Avenue. From those photos, Kesha knew that the area formed a perfect circle, with four evenly spaced darker lines extending from it. Landing gear, someone had suggested.

So now they had a clue; they had evidence. It was possible that everyone on earth hadn't just disappeared, that they hadn't simply vanished into thin air. Maybe they were taken away.

They should all be here right now, all the rebels. They should be combing the grass, climbing the trees, searching for more clues. They could be lighting bonfires, shooting fireworks, anything to draw attention to themselves. They could raid a television station, get their hands on satellite connections and communications equipment. Working together, they could figure out how to operate sophisticated technology. Cameron Daley was a real techie; he could come up with the means to relay messages and receive them, if anyone else was sending them. Okay, maybe it wouldn't be easy but they could be trying, they could be doing something.

As Kesha walked around the crushed grass she looked up into a blue, cloudless sky and felt so alone. She knew everyone thought of her as a confident young woman with a strong personality—some might say pushy—and an ambitious nature. But here, in the middle of this mystery, she was small and helpless. There was nothing she could do on her own.

She never thought she'd find herself alone like this. If no one else, her best friend should be here with her. But Donna had turned her back on the rebels to stay behind in the community. More specifically, to stay with Travis, in hopes of rekindling the relationship they once had. It wasn't much of a relationship, it never had been, and Kesha had thought Donna was over it. Sometimes, Kesha felt

Donna's betrayal was almost as much of a shock as the disappearance.

So who was left? She could write off the rest of the folks across the street in the hotel, Travis's group; they wouldn't help. They'd given up hope, all they wanted to do was survive. Even if they wanted to communicate with the rebels, Travis wouldn't let them. He'd posted guards who monitored their coming and going—for their own protection, he said. He'd convinced them that the rebels were misguided, possibly dangerous, and anxious to lure others into their anarchy. Maybe they *were* anarchists in a way, Kesha thought. They were just a handful of people, each with his or her own agenda.

Cam Daley was a smart guy, but he was more interested in his computer than in any human beings. She barely knew Adam Wise—he seemed okay, not a bad guy, just a blank. Alex and Shalini were interested only in each other. David Chu was both gorgeous and worthless, a party animal who stayed with the rebels solely because Travis's restrictions cramped his style.

Then there was Jake, their so-called leader. Kesha had admired Jake. She thought he had intelligence and a quiet courage, strength with sensitivity, determination tempered by a sense of humor. Who would have thought the departure of a girlfriend would put him in such a funk? Everyone had lost people—family, friends, boyfriends and girlfriends. They were all coping, why couldn't he? Ashley wasn't even one of the missing, she was just across the street with the community.

That was it, that was all of them. The eight rebels. They'd broken away from the community because they wouldn't accept that nothing could be done, because they wanted to know what happened to their world, and they wanted do something about it. But what were they doing? Moping, grieving, playing with computers. Nothing. Absolutely nothing.

She shivered involuntarily. It was colder now, and the knapsack was getting heavy. She turned away from the Great Lawn and started back downtown.